MW00721233

Any Resemblance to a Coincidence is Accidental

STEPHEN C. BIRD

Cover Design by Stephen C. Bird, Copyright © 2015
Illustrations by Stephen C. Bird, Copyright © 2015

Hysterical Dementia
ISBN 10: 0692347771
ISBN 13: 9780692347775

DISCLAIMER

In "Any Resemblance to a Coincidence is Accidental" – Many of names, pronouns and place names have been exaggerated by way of incorrect spellings. Verbs have been incorrectly conjugated as well. Most of these seemingly inaccurate spellings, and what appear to be grammatical errors, have been constructed intentionally – in a way that, for better or for worse, contributes to the elucidation of the author's point of view within this work. Although a few typographical errors will inevitably appear in any book, in "Any Resemblance to a Coincidence is Accidental", practically all of the misspellings of names, pronouns and place names -- as well as the incorrect conjugation of verbs -- have been carefully considered.

Stephen C. Bird, 2015

ACKNOWLEDGMENTS

See Endnotes

TABLE OF CONTENTS

.

TABLE OF CONTENTS

   Films, Books, Publications
   And TV Shows Referred To
   In "Any Resemblance To
   A Coincidence Is Accidental"

DEAR FAKEBOOK FIENDS
AND FRIENEMIES

Dear Fiendsters, Friendsters, Self-Haters, Low-Self Esteemers, Kiss-@ss Kassandras, Facetious Fascists, LinkedIn Losers, Nihilistic Narcissists, Prophetic Proselytizers, Voyeuristic Vamps, Black Market Oligarchs, Bored Rüm Beau-He-Mans, Emotionally-Disconnected Anti-Social-Networking Zombies: ..... I FORGOT WHAT THIS POST WAS SUPPOSED TO BE ABOUT! ..... I'm just kidding! Please don't get mad at me you guys! I love you all to death! And by *death* – I mean that good kind of *tarot* death! You guys are so great! Or at least that's what I tell all of my Fakebook fiends and frienemies – so that they'll stay my fiends and frienemies! Again – I'm just kidding! And all of you really are great – Like I said! You're fantastic!

1

This time I'm being sincere! I'm not telling you this just because I want to be liked! [..... *I believe* ..... *I think* ..... *I hope* .....] ..... I just have to cater to my Demon Within. That's what makes me a bitch, a hater – a faker! I mean, in my downtime when I'm not loving and respecting all of you!

Okay my beloved colleagues, from this point forward – no more kidding. From this point on – totally serious! This time I really MEAN it ..... Do you believe that I'm being flippant or sarcastic, in my half-hearted attempt to reveal to you the turbulent inner workings of my well-concealed emotional life? Good thing I don't give a flying fuck about what you think! By the way [or as they say on Fakebook – BTW] who came up with that expression – *flying fuck*? Since when can a *fuck fly*? Does it have something to do with aerodynamics? Or would it be physics? Is it a reference, in layman's terms, to the potential amount of energy contained within *a fuck*? Should I google *flying fuck*? Should I look it up on Wikipedia? Why not? No one reads books anymore. Everything has become so digitally impermanent – so apocalyptically Buddhist! But even more important than that ..... Fakebook destroyed friendship – and created FIENDSHIP and FRIENEMYSHIP! Fakebook provided us with an interface with which we can edit every spontaneous moment out of any personal interaction. The good news is this: If you happen to be a petty, vindictive, jealous competitive bastard like myself ..... then it probably makes you really happy when you get the chance to de-fiend or de-frienemy one of your Fakebook *associates*. That's right – Fakebook provides one with opportunities to practice *Schadenfreude!* Metaphorically speaking, you can place your fiend or frienemy in the *Star Trek Enterprise*[1] transporter and then beam them down – except there's no planet down below to beam them to! They'll just end up in the ether, in a vacuum ..... they'll rematerialize in a solar system on the outer orbit of a galaxy that itself is on the outside edge of a collection of galaxies contained within a multiverse. The de-fiended or the de-frienemied will then be trapped in *The Phantom Zone* like those villains from *Superman II*[2] ..... Which makes me so happy! Because I want to know that they'll be suffering.....

Before I go any further, there's something that I must tell you before I forget: Here's the world's most boring, most egotistical Fakebook post: "I HAD A VERY PRODUCTIVE DAY." Why not just say this instead: I WORK HARDER THAN ALL OF YOU LAZY FUCKS AND THAT MEANS I'M BETTER THAN YOU. SO WAKE UP AND SMELL THE POST-AMOURRICA PROFUNDAN STARFUCKS COFFEE AND MAYBE YOU'LL HAVE A CHANCE TO CATCH UP WITH ME BEFORE YOU'RE DEAD ..... Here's another suggestion: how about throwing some endearing self-deprecation into the mix and posting this instead: TODAY IS THE FIRST DAY OF THE REST OF MY LIFE – BUT UNFORTUNATELY I'VE DECIDED TO DO NOTHING FOR THE REST OF MY LIFE – BECAUSE I'M LOOKING FORWARD TO HAVING A MOUNTAIN OF REGRETS TO PONDER ON MY DEATH BED." I know ..... I should calm down ..... lighten up ..... take everything with a grain of salt. It's just that lately, and excuse me for using such a pedestrian expression .....

IF IT'S NOT ONE THING – IT'S ANOTHER. No one can be counted upon ..... Nonetheless, I will try to transcend my Bitter Bitch Within -- I'm just insecure because It's been so long since I posted on Fakebook. But even when I go on a Fakebook sabbatical ..... I can't let go of Fakebook. Fakebook has a hold on me, like an abusive lover that one keeps going back to – to be punched, degraded, denigrated, humili- ated ..... abandoned in a corner with a dunce cap on ..... whimpering like a wounded ani- mal. Fakebook doesn't treat me well, and yet I crave repeat episodes of that mistreatment ..... to continue the insanity. I keep checking the Fakebook Wall to see what I've missed, to see if I've made any new holographic fiends or frienemies. I check and I check ..... and all I end up getting are invitations from people who not even once, during the entire dura- tion of our Fakebook relationship, have ever taken a moment to LIKE one of my posts. And beyond that, should the Fakebook Deity permit me to speak so irreverently .... I've been living in absolute fear of Fakebook's Cowardly Not-So-New-Anti-World Department, that wants to sabotage my productivity by making me peruse advertisements for the latest gay fetish gear ..... that most of my gay fiends are not hot enough to wear. And even if they were ..... isn't it about time that my queer frienemies stopped objectifying each other ..... and finally did something constructive with their lives? Oh and BTW ..... did I neglect to tell you that I'm a *Real Girl*? I don't mean authentic – the concept of authenticity being so antiquated – I mean that I'm biologically a woman. And I'm an incredible fag hag, although not as imperiously intimidating as my girlfiend Jean-Nette the Jet Lag Fag Hag, who's so passive-aggressive that she'd rather laugh at me behind my back than speak to me. And for that ..... I worship her from afar. Okay I'm a hypocrite ..... I consider myself to be above posting on Fakebook and yet here I am doing it. I try to stay away and then when I start up again – I just can't stop! It's such an impossible battle -- like trying to destroy a Seven-Headed Hydra that keeps on sprouting *nuevas cabezas* that remind me constantly:

> ..... *You're not good enough to post on Fakebook .....everyone else is getting so skilled at posting, so polished, so professional, so eloquent ..... with their hip yet vaguely obscure references ..... don't pretend that those fiends and frienemies of yours don't have an ulterior motive ..... they've developed their competitive edge to the highest level ..... while you languish in obscurity ..... like that bitter loser poet in Satyricon[3] who was jealous of the successful yet mediocre poet .....*

BTW and as they say on Fakebook – *FYI* ["for your information"] – this whiny contradictory bitch has been busy. That's right, BUSY – as in having a real life off of Fakebook in the tangible, actual world. That's how I'm different from all of you guys. I know how to have fun; it's all so easy for me. I don't even have to try. People are drawn to me. No-one ever had to tell me

..... *let them come to you.* Because they always did. People trust me, I'm inherently trustworthy -- whereas I'll never trust anyone ..... In times of stress I've been known to recite the following prayers: *Universe please help me to love and to trust myself* ..... *Universe please help me to love and to trust others* ..... But it's not working ..... I know that you think I'm being condescending now. You think I'm acting like I'm better than you. But it's actually the opposite of that. It's my low self-esteem masked as arrogance. It's because I have nothing to say. It's because I'm a complete fraud, an absolute phony, and most of all – a total victim. My fiend-frienemies take me to parties and pass me around to be used as a punching bag for violent drunks. It's just like *Fight Club*[4] except for one major difference: I'm the only one who gets beat up. The aggressors call me *shit bag*, they call me *sack of shit* ..... and guess what? I want to be treated like shit because that's my fetish. It's all part of my latest master plan. Because if I get good enough at fetish – of the passive, submissive variety – then maybe my girlfiend Jean-Nette the Jet Lag Fag Hag will finally acknowledge my existence .....

But more on her later. It's time to check in with you. How are my words affecting you? Are you concerned? Are you planning an intervention on my behalf? Well before you do anything, know this: I don't want to be saved. I don't need your sympathy. I'm not looking to be rescued. I live in Brrrlin now – yes in Doucheyland! I actually have a passport ..... These Brrrliners have seen everything. I know, you think that all that they do – when they're not being incredibly efficient and using task-oriented methods to create a wide variety of practical, functional objects to contribute to the greening of the Blue Green Planet – is drink beer, smoke *in der Kneipe* and engage themselves in the leather-rubber-fetish lifestyle ..... well in one sense that is true ..... even the dumpiest of Brrrliners look like supermodels working their respective runways compared to those obese Amourrica Profundans! For instance -- the Brrrliners have no desire to see Parts One and Two of *Nymphomaniac*[5] – because they've already experienced everything referenced in those films. But seriously ...... the Brrrliners accepted the fact that perversion was a natural phenomenon long ago. Brrrlin bears little to no resemblance to the post Adolf Ghouliani, post Mikhail Gloomberg, Puta Jork, Nueva Jork. In Brrrlin there's no need for the Walk of Schäme, there's no need to sneak around in your dark sunglasses because you've been naughty ..... naughty is normal in Brrrlin. There's no need to hide beneath the artifice of an oppressive moral system ..... In that regard, check out this formula: *(1) Since fetish is natural; and (2) Since everything natural comes from nature, then (3) Fetish = Nature.* If I were a politician, that would be my slogan. I'm not politically correct, I'm not an activist and I've never been diplomatic. And although I'm more *voyeur than acteur* – here's an excerpt from one of my hypothetical campaign speeches:

FETISH EQUALS NATURE AND IF YOU CAN'T ACCEPT THAT THEN YOU'RE A STUPID REPRESSED FUCK WHO DOESN'T KNOW HOW TO HAVE

ANY FUN AND EVERYBODY'S LAUGHING AT YOU BEHIND YOUR BACK SO STOP LOOKING AT PORNOGRAPHIE AND JUST KILL YOURSELF ALREADY!!! AND SHOULD YOU CHOOSE TO DUST YOURSELF OFF AND REJOIN THE RAT RACE JUST LIKE EVERYONE ELSE WHO HATES THEIR GODDAMN LIFE THEN REMEMBER THIS: PERVER-SION IS A GOOD THING, YOUR WERE BORN PER-VERSE, YOU WILL ALWAYS BE PERVERSE ..... EVEN ONCE YOU'VE METAMORPHOSED BACK INTO STARDUST .....

In other words ..... stop pretending that you don't want to dress up as a Girl Scout and sell Girl Scout cookies to your 1950s-style Amourrica Profundan neighbors ..... that will be Step One of your downward spiral into fetish acclimation. Believe me – there are so many middle-aged men out there [who are not necessarily gay] who want to dress up as Girl Scouts. And let's not forget that *des gentilshommes d'un certain âge*, of whatever orientation, often want to dis-guise themselves as candy stripers. And not just on Halloween. I know ..... you're thinking ..... oh my Goddess [AKA "OMG"] -- Not another nurse in the Puta Jork, Nueva Jork Village Halloween Parade again! But I'm not talking about those bad girls who dress up as the classic fetish-influenced nurses – the ones that go topless with black electrical tape covering their nipples. I'm referring to the archetype of the innocent 1960s candy striper ..... the kind that your big sister used to volunteer as during high school or when she came home from college for summer vacation .....

I have a fetish for fetish! ..... BTW – Did you guys see *300: Rise of An Empire?*[6] Would it be wrong of me to refer to it as *PG Porn?* Now that I'm familiar with both of the *300*[7] movies – I don't need to watch porn anymore. I just watch the *300* films over and over. They're better than porn, because the sculpted warriors aren't completely naked – the eroticism is heightened due to that which is hidden! Besides *Xerxes I the God King* is so gay – in a really hot way! It's as if the best aspects of leather queen and drag queen were combined to form androgynous perfection! Xerxes reminds me of Mal-Hack, the metrosexual villain from Fan Crown's *In Search of The Boss Bimbo*. Okay ..... The God King is a little too pretty, yet he has this undeniably macho swagger, despite his being a total bitch. It's as if he's Joan Crawford in *Strait Jacket* combined with the essence of a queer stripper who works off-nights on the stage next to the DJ booth of the downstairs dance-floor of El Monstro, Puta Jork, Nueva Jork, Amourrica Profunda – the *Upstairs Downstairs* of gay bars! And then there's Artemisia – the anti-feminist feminist femme fatale antagonist of *300: Rise of An Empire* ..... in short, she fucks and she kills. Or at least she tries to seduce Themistocles, but she doesn't succeed and then Themistocles mortally wounds her with his sword. And finally – the real feminist hero of this drama is Queen Gorgo of Sparta. Gorgo doesn't waste her time trying to be sexy in some pretentious way ..... In spite of the symbolic possibilities contained within this film – don't take it too seriously. In the end – it's just a weekend-in-the-Poconos, heart-shaped tub kind of movie .....

gangsta-style ..... more *Heart-Shaped Box* than heart-shaped tub frankly. If you're bored during one of your *Fight Club*-style business trips – watch it in your hotel room .....

Not only haven't I posted on Fakebook since forever ..... I haven't posted in a while with words either. I usually post with photos because when I put up one of my inevitably fascinating verbal posts, I then have to deal with endless comments made by people who've misinterpreted what I've written ..... Did you know that everything I've been discussing up to this point is merely a minuscule excerpt from an infinitely longer draft of a Fakebook post that, were I to execute it, could result in a massive de-fiending ..... said de-fiending also being the result of a karmic payback for everyone that I've ever de-frienemied? Once I was blocked by Fakebook for a week for compulsively fiending *people who claimed that they didn't know me* ..... ALWAYS REMEMBER THIS: TO BE BLOCKED BY FAKEBOOK, FOR WHATEVER REASON, SHOULD BE CONSIDERED TO BE A BADGE OF HONOR. SO

THE NEXT TIME THAT THIS HAPPENS TO YOU .....
REVEL IN YOUR ANARCHIC MOMENT .....

I lived in Puta Jork for fifteen years and it took me the last ten years I was there to finally get the courage to leave! It changed for much ..... for the worse ..... many veteran Puta Jorkers are complaining about this. I thought about moving to Detroit; I took a trip there to check it out ..... Oh My Goddess – OMG -- What a dump! No thanks! ..... So I have no regrets about having moved to green, sexy and socialist Brrrlin ..... What reason does anyone have to live in Woman–Hattan, Puta Jork these days – besides having the opportunity to worship the Unholie Trinitie of Gaymart, Not-Right Aid and Duane Can't Read? Or to become the latest triple threat of the moment and to consequently shine as the toast of Fraud-Gay? Those are the only two reasons ..... You might as well just move to a less populated regional city, where you can experience the true horrors of the current Amourrica Profunda. All of you non-breeders will feel right at home in the smaller urban areas

– you'll find those Neo-Chelsea clones, who you once thought were so unique to Puta Jork, promenading along Beast Avenue, Rot-Fester, Nueva Jork. They're not so different from the clones in Woman-Hattan or Umsterdumb or Brrrlin. The only difference is their *accoutrements* – instead of an overpriced, undersized studio or a roommate in the Outer Bore-Hos – in Rot-Fester they'd rather own a fake Tudor house – complete with a weedless green lawn treated with Round-Down and bunny rabbits who consume the toxic leftovers. So light a fire under your lazy ass and get the hell out of your so-called hip zip code ..... unless you still take a fancy to strolling along West Fraud-Gay to check out the galleries, that are located on the ground floor of buildings containing five thousand dollar per month lofts, that feature works by the likes of LeRoi Knee-Woman. Just know that your hip zip code is the wrong zip code and that ..... THERE'S NO SUCH THING AS COOL / THERE'S NO SUCH THING AS HIP / AND THERE NEVER WAS. Cool is whatever you think is cool ..... *capisci? Hai capito?*

A Fakebook Rant About Fakebook

I WILL NOT BE YOUR VICTIM! DO YOU HEAR ME -- FAKEBOOK DEITY? GO FUCK YOUR MOTHER GODDESS – FAKEBOOK GOD! GO AHEAD AND KICK MY ASS! I'M NOT AFRAID OF YOU! ..... There's two sides to every story and the double edge of transcending the victim mentality is this: one risks the danger of turning into a gigantic, arrogant asshole! On the other hand, in situations where one feels threatened .... it's good to know that one's rage can be quickly summoned, like the proverbial genie (*djinni*) in a magic lamp. That being said – should one start to rely too heavily on this anger, be it sincere or manufactured ..... one risks alienating everyone around them. YES YOUR ANGER WILL FUNCTION AS YOUR WEAPON AGAINST FEAR – AS LONG AS YOUR ANGER DOESN'T BECOME A PROBLEM IN ITS OWN RIGHT ..... In closing, let me just say this: I'm not necessarily enamored of my rage, but I've definitely developed the ability to make a truce with that frienemy. These days, when I'm unlucky enough to find myself engaged in an interpersonal situation that's escalating into ugliness, I say to myself ..... *Just walk away from that creep ..... and go take a look in the mirror ..... to more thoroughly examine and come to terms with your own creep within* ..... *like the song says* ..... *"I'M A CREEP"* .....

Check out this text I wrote for my new Fakebook E-Card:

> *Don't Work for the Man – Don't Pass Go – Just Go to Jail!* [The complementary visual includes an illustration of Charles Woman-Son and those three notorious Woman-Son Girls with Xs on their foreheads. All four of the individuals represented in this image raise up their pinky and index fingers in the *sign of the horns*. The card is duotone; the background color is black; the text and the images are red.

Check out these posts that I'm working on! On any given day – I'll be laboring over three or four work-in-progress posts [I don't think the following material has any commercial viability -- so I'm just posting it for my Fakebook fiends and frienemies]. Okay here goes:

(1) *In the future, any Selfie [AKA "Selfishy"] receiving a minimum of five thousand (5000) LIKES will automatically be rewarded with the No-Bull Prize for Selfishies. However, due to this watering down of the credibility of the No-Bull Prize, certain winners – who consider their Selfishies to be more worthy of receiving a No-Bull Prize than those of their supposedly less talented counterparts – will challenge the allegedly inferior winners to a fight to the death: (a) in the manner of Celebrity Deathmatch[8]; or (b) in a style resembling the final days of the demise of the Rapa Nui culture of Easter Island .....*

(2) *I'm so far ahead of you people. I saw the first Higher Parterre film in Aqualung,*

Frenchyland in 1199. I read the first Higher Parterre book in a cave that I shared with a Knee-Andro-Gal tribe in Gee-Brawl-Tar twenty-four thousand years ago.

(3) *[Placeholder for a third post that I was commanded by Oksana the OCD Goddess to include – "to be determined" AKA "TBD"].*

BTW FYI – I'm writing my memoir! You're never too young to write a memoir! [Better hurry up and write your memoir before the Grim Reaper cuts you down!] However if you're strapped for time – or if you think your life is boring – then write a MINIMOIR. Thanks to this new category of literature – people won't be expecting too much! The best part of all is this: you don't even have to write a *minimoir* -- and the reader doesn't have to read it – all of the pages are blank .....

Check out these posts from one of my Fakebook frienemies – Danny Diprivan! I don't ever want to meet this fiend in person – but I sure like the things that he writes!

(1) This FeignBook – it's just a numbers game with vanity, narcissism, self-indulgence and self-promotion ruling the roost! Besides – the quality of my fiend and frienemy list is so much more interesting on SpaceGrave! I don't care if everyone says that SpaceGrave is dead! On SpaceGrave one can find underground punk rock drag queens from Lost Angelist, Kali-Porn-Eye-Ay and Brrrlin, Doucheyland; Goths from the Disunited Queendom ..... anarchists from Umsterdumb! Whereas on FazeBook it's just people posting pictures of their babies and cats! You'll never find a purple profile page covered with grinning orange pumpkins on FeignBook! SpaceGrave is so much more visual – not to mention visceral! I'm so sorry that the template for SpaceGrave had to be appropriated and then gentrified to become FazeBook!! The format of FeignBook can

be compared to that of an Excel spread-
sheet, or to that of a PowerPoint presentation, both of which were created for
use in Corporate Bored Rüms ..... So fiend
me on SpaceGrave and then I'll harass
you with deluge after deluge of flyers for
events that I produce – because I want
you to COME TO MY THING! That being
my circa 1973 black light heavy metal
glitter parties! Just don't expect me to
attend your event! I'm too busy to have
any fun! When you've become as high
profile as me -- then I'll come and check
out your show ..... In the meantime – I
want to blow up bridges! I hate stabil-
ity! The fires of Woodstock 1999 will burn
forever in my heart. The community that
I've created lacks integrity – because
integrity doesn't exist! Chaos / Anarchy
/ Destruction = Dionysian BadBook! Or
how about Strip Mall Opium of the Masses
Apollonian GoodBook? Depending on
whether your see the glass half empty or

hall full ..... FazeBook isn't *Future Shock* – It's *Future Numb!* And why do people think I want to see pictures of their dirty dishes! Why not just take a shit on a plate and post it as *mousse au chocolat!* [Oh so you think just because I'm vulgar That I'm too dumb to know any French? – Just kidding you guys!] ..... I've finally decided to rid myself of this multitude of worthless frienemyships! My FeignBook fiendship list cleanup is continuing. Down from a high of 4,999 to 3,999. Not pulling any punches ..... more dominoes will have to fall! If we communicate hardly ever, and by *we* – I mean most of you – you're in danger of being de-frienemied. I know – It hurts! But someone has to pay. You've been warned. Just remember this: however you choose to deal with this rejection – don't go on Google Plus! Here's why:

Google Plus exists in cyberspace as an empty, ghostly villa ..... whose elegant fur-

niture ….. that had its origins in an extinct aristocracy ….. has been covered with dusty gray, beige and pale blue sheets …..

(2) *I don't want to think about death! I'm too young! I'll save that for later – just like everyone else! Nonetheless, here's the inscription that I'd like to see on my grave-stone – when I'm looking down upon it from heaven:*

My plastic surgery was spiritually moti-vated. I instructed the surgeon to fol-low the Four Directions of the Native Amourrican Universe with his scalpel …..

FAKEBOOK FAKEGIRL CODA

And now I'd like to tell you about a fiend-fri-enemy of mine who's going through some hard times. He's not from a poor family, he's not on drugs and his drinking is manageable [thanks to his vanity, none of his vices have turned into addictions]. His name is Noloso Chushingura. He's a guy who's achieved very little in life, aside from being a slut, and he's not even any good at that. But attempting to be promiscuous always got him out of the house and away from a possibly permanent and life-threatening depression. He started to feel like a failure after his second mid-life crisis. And so he decided to leave Puta Jork, Nueva Jork, his adopted city of thirty-three years. He'd moved there, with a pocketful of dreams at the age of twenty, to attend Nueva Jork University as a theatre major. He dropped out with one semester to go before graduation -- and you know why that is? BECAUSE HE NEVER HAD ANY FUCKING BALLS! HE COPPED OUT EVERY CHANCE THAT HE GOT! THERE'S SO MUCH HE COULD HAVE ACHIEVED IF HE'D ONLY HAD THE NERVE TO SHOW UP! He was never even aggressive enough to have a temper tantrum in his high chair. WHAT AN IMPOTENT DICKLESS EUNUCH .....

I feel so sad about Noloso even though I'm being harsh in the way that I describe him. But

I had to drop him as a real-life fiend-frienemy, because to know him was to actively partici-pate in my own self-sabotage. He was inter-esting – I'll grant him that. BUT DID YOU EVER NOTICE HOW INTERESTING PEOPLE NEVER HAVE ANY FUN? YOU KNOW WHY? BECAUSE THEY'RE TOO AFRAID TO LEAVE THE HOUSE ..... THEY SPEND HOURS OCCUPYING THEMSELVES WITH ENDLESS OCD RITUALS ..... Noloso is a person that had so much potential, a person who wasted his life, a person that no one has ever understood. And just because people don't understand you ..... doesn't mean that you possess greatness .....

MUCHA NIEVE AND MIASMA FALLS

Noloso Chushingura Returns To Mucha Nieve

..... *He wandered the streets nearby the Smellicott Bus Station in downtown Mucha Nieve, Nueva Jork. Dressed in black, dirty, displaced. He collected cans and bottles in a shopping cart that he then took to the supermarket – and that's how he supported himself ..... Although he could survive this way – it was a stressful lifestyle that exacerbated his already delicate state of physical and mental health. He would curse at passersby under his breath in a thwarted effort to connect to his fellow man. And he relished that experience as his anger made him feel powerful ..... A person like this, abandoned by the world, becomes resourceful and discovers many surprising uses for discarded plastic bags. And this gives that individual street cred* .....

Noloso was just his nickname – a dyslexic, abbreviated version of The Not-So-Lovable Loser. He'd moved back to Mucha Nieve with the wrong set of expectations; no expectations at all would have been preferable. But then his entire reason for relocating had self-destructive origins. Shortly before vacating his Puta Jork, Nueva Jork apartment, he'd unexpectedly received a letter in the mail informing him that he'd won a full scholarship for a six-month program at *El Instituto de Clown del Tierra Del Fuego* ["The Clown Institute of Tierra Del Fuego]" in Patty Phoney-Yeah, Archie-Bettyna, Sud Amourrica Profunda. This new opportunity had dropped from the heavens *deus ex machina* style. But like so many other chances that had come his way ..... he rejected it, he said that he didn't want it ..... When in truth, he might as well have pursued it, because he was in desperate need of a purposeful existence.....

After his homecoming, he stayed for a week at his mother's apartment in a gated community for seniors in the suburbs. He then moved to Palin-Town, Mucha Nieve's sorry excuse for a Beau-He-Man neighborhood and home to many an *Eerie Countie Faerie*. Noloso had very little experience driving an automobile, since he'd never owned a car during his years in Puta Jork. And now he was faced with having to get around in a primarily blue-collar, car-oriented city where hockey, beer, chicken wings and a casual, substratum Midwest provincialism held sway. At first glance, Palin-Town appeared to be charming with its gently sloping side streets and well-appointed homes. But it didn't take long for Noloso to realize that every third house was occupied by either drug dealers or prostitutes, to which the lawyers and doctors, who lived on either side of them -- had apparently turned a blind eye ..... Ill-kempt, shadowy neighborhoods would suddenly run up against areas featuring Italianate, Vicktorian and Greek Revival-style homes, all of them with electric Christmas candles glowing in their street-facing windows. The streetlights of Mucha Nieve burned too harshly at night, as if they were interrogation lamps waiting to illuminate would be criminals. After midnight, even on the thoroughfares of its swankier neighborhoods -- there was nary a soul on foot to be seen. Everyone seemed to be in hiding, especially due to the severe winter .....

After arriving at his short-term rental apartment in Palin-Town, Noloso decided to go out for a walk in the brutal cold and freshly fallen snow from the latest blizzard – to get some perspective on his current environs. He proceeded northward on Elf-Would Avenue from Venerea Street, crossing Dead-Ward Street and then passing the Quarter-Dollar Store on the way to Palin Street. And the people that he saw and heard along the way were the hostile disenfranchised characters of a quasi-ghetto ..... Among Amourrica Profundan cities with a population of more than two hundred and fifty thousand – Mucha Nieve was the fifth poorest in the nation; it also counted itself among the top ten most segregated Amourrica Profundan municipalities. Most of the whites lived to the west of Mainstream Street and the blacks lived to the east; Palin-Town, however, appeared to be proportionally integrated. The folks that Noloso passed by were either unaware of, or unconcerned with, anything that existed beyond the borders of their town. They were black; they were Hispanic; they were white, they were chartreuse, they were vermilion ..... they were drunk; they were angry; they were in denial; they were disturbed. They all looked down and out. They engaged in heated discussions concerning their imminent survival that had the potential to explode and disturb the peace at any given moment. They sang Spanish rap songs angrily under their headphones; they sang popular ballads loudly and slightly off key. And those songs functioned as a warning that said ..... *stay the fuck away from me, to know me is to be hated by me, I'd just as soon kill you as look at you* ..... These urban characters, who made up this multi-spectral and multi-cultural mosaic, were the kind of people that caused affluent suburbanites shake in their boots; that prompted them to look both ways before they jumped into their Audis and Porsches to zoom back out to their cozy, spacious homes; to their Republican majority villages; to their ski chalets; to their pottery stores. They'd commute into the city to attend cultural events in tony pockets of the hollowed out urban shell that was Mucha Nieve .....

To find the motivation to escape from his longtime adopted-hometown of Puta Jork, Nueva Jork – the city that had formed his character; the metropolis that he'd made his own – Noloso hit upon the following visualization ..... *he was standing on one of the floating islands of Avatar[9] ..... high in the sky. He was pushing his fifth floor junior one bedroom (translation: shoebox) apartment off of the cliff-like edge of the floating island. He watched his former dwelling fall, from the topmost layer of Pan-War-Uh's noxious atmosphere, the distance of that downward trajectory being so far ..... so deep .... that its impact with the surface below was imperceptible .....* After a lifetime of screaming at open mikes, at poetry readings in cafés, in the dark basements of Irish bars or before small to non-existent audiences in storefront *Way Off Fraud-Gay* theaters

— Noloso had returned to lick his wounds in his *Cave of Sorrows* in Mucha Nieve, also known as *The City of Not-So-Good Gay Bars* or *The Closet Queen City* [ominous-present Reign-Beau Flags notwithstanding] ..... To the north, south and east of Mucha Nieve's municipal borders were, respectively, the suburbs of Taanaawaanaa, Laackaawaanaa and Chicktaawaagaa. Noloso had grown up in the posh suburb of Beast of Aura about half an hour south of Mucha Nieve, just north of Dumb-Fuck and Smellicottville. At age nineteen, after finally having acquired his driver's license, he began to drive downtown to frequent Mucha Nieve's LGBTQ scene. By his mid-thirties he'd become bored with the provincial Mucha Neveano gay bars that he'd patronize during holiday visits to his parents. His favorite club, *Mean Phallus*, had been shut down in the early Eighties in the wake of the AIDS crisis .....

Noloso had to face it. The now gentrified, Disneyfied Puta Jork, Nueva Jork had turned him into a cream puff. In his own mind, he was right back where he'd started from, just as naïve as he'd been when he moved to Puta Jork at the age of twenty. He'd ended up being intimidated by the latest twenty- and thirty-something generation of Puta Jork; the harmless-looking *business bitch careerists* of either sex; the Machiavellian corporate climbers disguised as faux-neo-hipsters ..... Conversely, even if the Mucha Neveanos' Amourrica Profoundan dream hadn't already turned into a nightmare ..... the unglamorous, unvarnished quality of life in a smaller regional municipality -- like that of humble Mucha Nieve -- was much easier to detect than was the case in a gigantic megalopolis like Puta Jork. Because in Mucha Nieve -- there were simply fewer places where Ugly Reality could hide ..... And so Noloso pondered ..... *these Mucha Neveanos are the people who've put their dreams on hold, or who've acted like they've never had any dreams ..... they've accepted the lives that they believed themselves to have chosen, not even realizing that they've compromised, because they've never traveled outside of Eerie Countie, Nueva Jork to see what lay beyond its borders. They* love their city even though it's the only one that they've ever known .....

Noloso didn't belong here, but then he didn't belong anywhere. There was nothing ahead of him but clouds of black and the darkest of grays ..... He felt distressed and sought help from above. And so he prayed to Maya Hiyuh Powuh ..... *Bring me Laura Palmer as Glinda the Good in Wild At Heart ..... and if she's not available, bring me green-faced Elf-Abba from Weak-Ed ..... I reserve much love for brown as well as green -- though I've always been hated for my frank discussion of the color shit brown – that was never featured in Crayola crayon boxes of any size ..... Okay Elf-Abba is no Margaret Hamilton, but should she decide to ride on her broomstick in the sky above me and write "Surrender Noloso" as she goes .... I will concede ..... Because I've never been able to make decisions ..... I'll acquiesce as soon as I'm commanded to do so ..... Everything that I'm fright-ened of will be channeled into my work-in-prog-ress entitled "Self-Hatred for Dummies: Anarchic*

Dissipation and Enforced Invisibility".   Here's an excerpt from that upcoming work:

> *Go out and enjoy yourself! Forget about being "An Accomplished Individual Worthy of Respect"! Forget about creating anything noteworthy or about making meaningful contributions to the various incompatible cultures of the Blue Green Planet ….. and to the civilizations that may arise thereafter ….. Oh Maya Hiyuh Powuh ….. Only Miss Lonelyhearts from Rear Window[10] can empathize with my pain ….. if the Goddess does not hear and respond to my prayers, I may go into seclusion, to become a shut-in who does nothing but watch Juliet of the Spirits[11] repeatedly, just as I did during my second mid-life crisis (which lasted eons longer than the first one) ….. Speaking of Oi-Ropean filmmakers, the collage-style of Muriel[12] has always reminded me of films that we used to watch in the auditorium of Fart-Smell Hell-Ementary School, Beast of Aura, Nueva Jork in the late 1960s. Whether in color or in black and white ….. even educational movies made for*

children had verve and panache back then …..
although my major influences from that decade
were my brother's and sister's respective psyche-
delic record collections …..

Noloso nursed a dark fascination with fairy tales, specifically those featuring princesses and sorceresses. As a child he'd learned how to block out reality with *Sleeping Beauty*[13]. He'd held onto the 1957 storybook version that he'd scribbled in as a child -- for most of his adult life. That book had survived his various moves around the Bore-Hos of Puta Jork, but in the process it had become damaged and had had to be disposed of. Luckily he'd managed to find a used copy of that very same book, in mint condition, on EBay. He purchased it for twelve dollars. Surely the previous owner had been unaware of the value of this superlative work, to have given it away for a steal ….. Noloso lost himself in the colors of the lush backgrounds. What drew him in were the pinks, blues, aquas, olives, yellows, purples and blacks. He wished that he could disappear into those meticulously illustrated landscapes that had been so ingeniously rendered by the Disney Studios team, who'd worked at the peak of their powers in 1950s Amourrica Profunda. Noloso's mother suspected that this obsession with *Sleeping Beauty* involved his blossoming artistic side, but it was much more than that. Noloso didn't identify with the prince, but rather with the princess. He knew that he'd been drawn to men since the age of seven, when he'd become acutely aware of his attraction to the physique of Adam [*Michael Parks*] in *The Bible: In The Beginning*[14]. Beyond that, he'd actually suffered from a sexual confusion whereby he felt strongly feminine ..... to the point where he'd considered a sex change. Forty years later, he finally came to the realization that the physiology of his being, as well as his overall essence, tilted towards the masculine. From age thirteen onwards, he'd always imagined himself as the bottom in his fantasy life ..... the passive / receptive role was what he most closely associated with antiquated stereotypes of women who were yielding and submissive; generalities that he could readily absorb into his closeted existence, as the qualities of the quintessential gay male of the 1970s were still strongly associated with the feminine .....

Similarly to Bob Fosse, as the protagonist in *All That Jazz*[15] – Noloso wondered ..... *Maybe I'm not so weird after all ..... perhaps I'm just like those people that I made fun of while growing up ..... the ones that spoke with the flat A's and the heavily nasal tone of the Eerie Countie accent. Why should I think I'm any better than some cashier at Tops ..... or even Wegmans [the classier supermarket of the two]? I've been fired from every job that I ever had ..... Still -- Mommy always liked the way that I combined the pretty colors in my childhood artwork. She recognized my potential as a visual artist, a career that has yet to materialize ..... It's all my fault since I never believed that I could handle the pressure of going to the next level, of making it in the big time ..... I could never adjust to the idea of creativity being a "job". And while we're on the subject ..... Monty-Sorry Clift should have stayed in his hometown of Oma-Pa, Nebulaska, Fartland, Amourrica Profunda. No one would know his name now – but wouldn't he have been better off existing there as a supermarket cashier – than as a decadent, unhappy movie star mixing crushed pills in a thermos filled with grapefruit and vodka? Helen Lawson had a point when she informed Neely O'Hara in "Valley of The Dolls"[16]: "Fraud-Gay doesn't go for booze and dope" ..... [Noloso fell into a "trance within a trance" and proceeded to impersonate Neely O'Hara] ..... "So what if that fag Ted Caasaablaankaah made a million dollars in 1966! Even if he was such a fabulous queen ..... think of all the other bitches whose nails he must have stepped on as he clawed his way to the top" .....*

Noloso snapped out of his daydream. It was a clear cold Siberian night and the moon was full. He walked uptown past the northwest corner of Elf-Would Avenue and Whore Street. He was heading towards Price Fight, a middle-grade supermarket. But Price Fight closed at nine in the evening, too early for a night owl like himself. So he stepped into Aahmaar's "Puta Jork-Style Deli" to buy a cup of coffee. Noloso was dressed in Timberland boots,

Adidas sweatpants, a North Face jacket, synthetic thermal underwear, a Burton Snowboards black winter cap and a generic, green oversized hoodie that he'd purchased in Chinatown, Puta Jork, Nueva Jork. People tended to avoid him ..... even though he was more afraid of them than they were of him. He could make eye contact with folks as they walked past ..... but he was like a cat that would freeze, arch its back or run up a tree in a panic at the slightest provocation. He'd developed a bitter, hard look, as well as outlook, after years of failed relationships during his time in Puta Jork. And with no awards, accolades, notable achievements, or even a gift for maintaining conventional employment to his credit, he in no way felt superior to any of the displaced degenerates of Elf-Would Avenue. He used his humor for diplomatic purposes; it functioned as a screen for his barely concealed hostility that threatened to unravel any of his tenuous connections to the human race .....

Noloso walked one block downtown on Elf-Would Avenue and then turned left, going east towards Hell-Aware Avenue on Palin Street. He crossed Hell-Aware to go to the gas station convenience store on the southeast corner of Palin and Hell-Aware. But there was a long line of people inside who'd apparently come out of hibernation after the latest snowstorm. So he decided instead to walk one block north to Wall-Greeds on the southwest corner of Hell-Aware and Whore. He carefully navigated the lumps of refrozen snow under his feet on the way. Once he'd reached the Theo-War Bozo-Smell Historic Site on the southeast corner of Whore and Hell-Aware, he was greeted by a group of hooligans who were gathered around a crackling bonfire in front of that memorial. These squatters were laughing, cursing and shrieking as they danced and jumped around the blaze. What was the inspiration for their sadistic merriment? The entire scenario brought to mind medieval villagers letting off steam in *Robin Hood: Prince of Thieves*[17] ..... It turned out that this group had just sacrificed a local girl by the name of Dusty Trust Fund. Dusty represented everything that the hooligans were not. They were the have-nots whereas Dusty had it all. Dusty had been a straight A student in high school. She'd grown up on tony Farthingham Terrace in Douchebag, Nueva Jork in the western Cats-Kills. After graduation she'd relocated to Puta Jork to realize her artistic dreams. Once in Puta Jork, she'd started to associate with a shady crowd and had ended up doing crack and crystal meth; she'd also engaged in prostitution and some low-end pornography. *So much promise wasted* ..... the downcast eyes of her parents seemed to say when they spoke of the daughter that they hadn't seen in years. Dusty had lost everything – her self-worth, her self-esteem, her potential for personal and financial value. Given her desperate situation, she'd moved to Mucha Nieve with an abusive boyfriend; they ended up living in a rundown three-story Vicktorian on Vie-Fagra Street that had been taken over by local riff-raff. Dusty had actually been very popular with her newfound peers, until they found out that she came from money. She didn't have access to the funds; she'd severed all ties with her bourgeois family. But no matter. Her connection to opulence had been established. And since it had been revealed that she was a child of privilege, she'd have to pay the price ..... That night, Dusty's quasi-*Symbionese Liberation Army* / pseudo-*Der Baader Meinhof Complex*[18] house-mates committed the ultimate act of betrayal. They awoke her from a deep sleep and then bound and gagged her. Her mouth was strapped shut with silver electrical tape; both her wrists and her ankles were fastened together with black duct tape. She was then dumped into the back seat of a rusted-out 1977 pine green Chevy Nova and driven from the Vie-Fagra Street residence to the Theo-War Bozo-Smell Historic Site. On the front lawn of that property, Dusty was beaten to death. She was then set aflame upon a funeral pyre in preparation for her descent into Anti-Valhaha. As she burned, her squatter peers sang songs to celebrate the demise of this rich bitch that they'd decided to use as their scape-goat ..... No passersby or motorists stopped to intervene and the cops were too busy, as Mucha Nieve was vastly underserved by its police force. Coincidentally on that night, the city was abuzz with an unusually high rate of criminal activity in more dangerous areas to the east and south of Palin-Town. And even if the cops had bothered to investigate the sacrifice of Dusty, they probably would have sided with her killers. Her parents weren't surprised by her fate. *Dusty played with fire ..... and those that play with fire will be burned .....* they intoned with moral superiority as they stood in front of the living room bay window of their suburban mansion, gazing out at the brilliant winter sunset preceding *le crépuscule* ..... As soon as he'd witnessed this disturbing ritual, Noloso picked up his pace. He desired no truck with these *Omega Man*[19]-esque *Creatures of The Night*. When danger threatened, when menace was in the air – the lone wolf moved on to sniff out safer territory .....

Noloso was shaken by the demise of Dusty Trust Fund and he needed a drink. So he decided to trek over to Palin Street and buy a twenty-four ounce can of LaFrack's Brew, a Kanuckyan beer popular in Eerie Countie (Kanuckya was Amourrica Profunda's *Slightly Less Repressed /*

Slightly More Socialistic Neighbor to the north). He scurried west along Whore Street, crossed Elf-Would Avenue and then turned left onto Woolworth Street. He continued on to the end of Woolworth, which curved to the left and became Palin Street. He then stepped into the nearby Bally-Would Farms Bodega to purchase a LaFrack's Brew. When he came out of the store, he was visited by a vision as he negotiated the icy, corrugated sidewalks on the way back to his Palin-Town short-term rental apartment .....

..... In the darkroom of Beast of Aura High School, which one gained access to by means of the science department, which was located in an open space suffering from an excess of harsh fluorescent lighting, due to its lack of windows ..... Noloso was approached by a man who appeared as a silhouette before the darkroom entrance. The man proceeded to address him in a Doucheylandish accent: "Since I'm light years ahead of you,

please listen to my advice ..... Stay here in this small backwater town where you grew up looking forward to church bells chiming on blue sky whistling wind Sunday spring mornings, where you could listen to a priest deliver a sermon that subliminally extolled the virtues of the Protestant Twerk Ethick ..... I think that would be more your speed. I know that you resent me for being yet another authority figure that you must contend with. But I'm actually doing you a favor. Remain in the village of your upbringing and do something productive with your life. Do volunteer work or reinvent yourself as the local eccentric. Start your own stained glass window business ..... at any rate, these days you can be ninety-nine percent gay in a small Amourrica Profundan town. You won't have that kind of decadent fun that you'd find in Umsterdumb or Brrrlin. But you can get married to another man, move into a delightful bungalow and then adopt a baby. You can drink chamomile tea in the evenings and read all of the major works of the Western Canon. Don't be a loser sack of Scheiße -- there's still time to save yourself. Just think of me as your Jacob Marley who's come to warn you. Now let's get going with your spiritual quest .....

..... Then Noloso was in the Dalai-Would The-atre in Folly-Would, Lost Angelist, Kali-Porn-Eye-Ay. He'd just won a Hieronymus Boscar for Best Obscene Design. His acceptance speech ran the gamut of emotions. There were tears of joy intermingled with jokes; there was so much that he wanted to say before his time ran out ..... he thanked Maya Hiyuh Powuh for help-ing him to get through all of those suicidal moments and back into his Vein of Gold[20] ..... those being the rare intervals of sunshine that returned him to the joy of creation ..... Suddenly an Occupy Folly-Would protester stormed the stage and tried to wrestle Noloso's cherished Boscar away from him; a struggle ensued and in a rage-filled panic, Noloso beat the protester to death with his statuette ..... Noloso spent the

rest of his life in prison writing violent screenplays and making refrigerator drawings; his works featured protagonists of the Tennessee Williams variety à la Sebastian Venable, the "Hothouse Flower" of Suddenly Last Summer[21]. But Noloso was versatile and when he wasn't fending off sexual assaults by psychopathic tattooed musclemen, he cranked out a novelization of Frank Catheter's "It's A Not-So-Wonderful Shit Life". In this new and improved version of that classic film, in the scene describing the dance at the high school gym ..... instead of falling into the swimming pool, the characters tumble into the downward flowing waters of the southernmost 9-11 Memorial ..... the base of which metamorphoses into the bottomless pit of "300" .....

Noloso knew that he was done with Amourrica Profunda. He'd decided to escape to Kanuckya and to permanently avoid jury duty for the rest of his life. He would cross the border and travel to Fart Eerie, Bomb-Scary-O, Kanuckya. At customs, he'd state to the border agent that he'd be visiting a friend in Fart Eerie, when in fact he'd planned on settling down in Creep River, a desolate town that lay halfway between Grimmsbie and Stoner Creek, about eighty kilometers further northwest. Counter-culturally speaking ..... Creep River was so goth, so avant-garde, so beatnik, so beau-he-man and so underground – that it was known to no-one else on the Blue Green Planet besides Noloso. He checked out of his Palin-Town short-term rental apartment and then took a cab to the Middle Earf Frampton Inn Hotel in downtown Mucha Nieve. He would stay there for one night and then depart for Kanuckya the next day. After checking in and leaving his suitcase in his room, he walked over to the Smellicott Bus Station, a notorious landmark in downtown Mucha Nieve's *Skid Row*. As he entered the station, a druggy-looking couple à la *Natural Born Killers* were sitting outside smoking ..... The Smellicott Station featured an odd cross-section of the multi-faceted Amourrica Profundan demographic. Among the customers found in the waiting room were the Amish (*AKA*

"*Amiszcz*"); the Amiszcz women wore black nine-teenth century-style prairie bonnets, black capes and sensible black shoes; the bearded Amiszcz men, with their bowl-haircuts and wide-brimmed black hats, wore royal blue dress shirts under-neath their black vests and black jackets. In the center of the station, standing by an easel fea-turing a poster, were what at first appeared to be well-dressed businessmen ..... who upon closer inspection revealed themselves to be Jehovah's Witnesses. There were black men socializing at the tables in front of Tiny Tim Whore-Ton's who weren't waiting for busses – but rather seeking refuge from the cold. The bus station men's room / *tea room* was a haven for *down-low* activity; a phenomenon that Noloso had frequently expe-rienced in his *been there, done that* lifestyle ..... Noloso proceeded to the counter to purchase a ticket for Fart Eerie. There was only one customer ahead of him; a guy wearing a camouflage jacket and army fatigues who looked like he'd lived a hard life. Diagonally to Noloso's right was a tough-looking white cop, close shaven

and / or bald, sporting the classic dark blue out-
fit with a firearm in his holster; in a former life he
may have had a career with the World Wrestling
Federation. The policeman and the heavy-set
black male ticket agent were enjoying a con-
spiratorial work time chat. The ticket agent
wrapped up the conversation and addressed
Noloso:

Ticket Agent:
Can I help you?

Noloso:
Yes I'd like to purchase a ticket for Fart Eerie for
tomorrow.

Ticket Agent:
What time would you like to leave?

Noloso:
Just give me the departure times please and I'll
pick the one that's best for me.

Ticket Agent (*becoming exasperated*):
How about you just tell me when you'd like to leave?

Noloso:
The professional thing to do would be to tell me the departure times.

Ticket Agent (*adamant*):
We're not going to go through all that.

Noloso (*hesitating, resigned*):
Is there a departure at 2 pm?

Ticket Agent:
That'll work. Twenty dollars please.

Noloso (*casually*):
Why are you being rude to me?

Ticket Agent:
I'm not being rude to you.

Noloso (pointedly):
You seem angry.

Ticket Agent:
I'm not angry.

Noloso (*slyly*):
Well, we all have our problems and issues, don't we?

Ticket Agent (*ignoring Noloso's comment*):
Your bus will leave from gate 4.

Noloso was upset. The ticket agent had dealt with him as if he were vermin. The agent had been either completely unaware of his hostile behavior -- or calculatingly callous. Noloso would have told the ticket agent off in different circumstances. But he was dissuaded by the presence of the scary-looking cop with the firearm. As Noloso left Smellicott Station, he passed by the *Natural Born Killers*[22] couple; they were stoned on something and the female of the pair smiled disturbingly. He then walked back to the Middl Earf Frampton Inn Hotel, avoiding eye contact with the sketchy characters that he met in passing .....

The Dark Angel
Of Blue Silence
Who Speaks To
Noloso Chushingura
During His Rem Sleep
[El Angelo Oscuro
Del Silencio Azul]

You wish that you could experience gay life as a man who truly belongs to the tribe. You are an observer who treads water out in the depths, beyond that party palace on a festive strip of sand that has never embraced you, because you yourself refused to bring anything to the table. You set yourself apart – you watched from afar. You wish that you could accept and experience the politically correct aspect of the queer milieu. You're still repulsed by the drag queens, the leather studs and the pretty boys because they remind you of that clique of kids in high school who were the most popular. And in the context of this kind of subculture that is so prevalent in LGBTQ life – they have indeed ended up being the most popular. These homo archetypes are incredibly cynical; yet they admit to no cynicism. These amalgams of myriad "what used to be considered underground" queer subcultures try so hard to be cutting edge; they are a parody of an avant-garde that never existed in the first place. The homo underworld devours the detritus of the Kuiper Belt of mainstream breeder culture and then vomits the waste back up as a gigantic, grotesque, partially developed fetus. Because in today's world there's no longer time for either gestation or digestion. Instead, there are only visceral, knee jerk reactions inspired by a complete lack of reflection …..

C'mon you know that you want to be in with the in crowd ….. surrender to Elf-Abba's green smoke broom! Just lobotomize yourself with an overdose of crystal meth ….. all of your teeth will fall out and your cock sucking abilities will soar!

Stop thinking so much and the number of friends that you have will increase exponentially. No one cares about your brain; no one's going to remember you when you die..... all that you'll be is one more person who struggled with reality in a futile attempt to delay your eventual decomposition into stardust ..... What have you done with your life? You who are so busy getting nothing done ..... as you inhale deeply from the lingering ether of a Prozac Ecstasy Viagra cocktail .....

Did you know that I participated in a number of Twelve Step groups before I gave myself enough credit to become a Sexually Indeterminate Goddess who goes by the name of "Fräulein Faschistin"? And so vwaalaah – here's Fräulein Faschistin's suggestion: Get yourself over to your local bookstore and buy yourself a copy of my brilliant colleague Fräulein Furzen's "How to Stop Slut Shaming Yourself" (the original Doucheyland / Eye-Talian title is as follows: "Die Schlamperella Della Motzstraße"). That'll be your ticket to increased clarity and serenity. Forget Pal-Anon! Those people are a bunch of sad sacks. Here are some other books I'd recommend for wounded whimpering self-pitying animals like yourself:

(1) "How to Make a Business Plan for Your Downward Spiral"

(2) "How to Destroy your Potential for Achieving Anything Noteworthy"

(3) "How to Finally Realize that The Pursuit of Success, Notoriety and Happiness is Futile"

BTW FYI – If all else fails and you're unable to turn off the chattering of your sociopathic voices, then pray to the Universe -- even if you see this Universe only as a scientific concept that happens to complement your Buddhist neutrality. FAKE IT TILL YOU FAKE IT MORE – JUST LIKE YOU DO ON FAKEBOOK. Then you'll finally be free from any obligation of reverence for all of those institutions that your parents taught you to respect ….. your schools; your monotheistick organizations; your state and federal Govern-Meants. Just remember this ….. you're going to be lonely in your void; remember Mimi Rogers at the end *of "The Rapture"?[23] ..... That's what's going to happen to you ..... No one ever said that being completely untethered from mainstream social structures and networks would be easy ..... you who will finally break free from the chains of your so-called secular humanist commitments ..... to realize that the abyss in its non-philosophical form is no picnic .....*

SOVIET UNION THRIFT STORE

PAVLINA PERESTROIKA

Just as Noloso Chushingura had disappeared into the Bally-Would Farms Bodega, Pavlina Perestroika was bumping on down Palin Street towards Woolworth Street with a swish that belied the effects of middle age upon her ravaged, hardened face. She wore a cocoa-beige pleather jacket and a tacky stone wash denim skirt with corduroy patches. Pavlina reveled in the cool colors of the blue jay – as well as in the brownish tones of the female cardinal. Her look resembled the couture of a Soviet Union thrift shop circa 1983. Ultimately her entire wardrobe could be categorized as *pre-glasnost nostalgie*. Pavlina was morose, realistic and she kept her complaints to a minimum. Amourrica Profunda was the only country that she was ever going to know and that was just fine with her. She knew inherently that people were the same everywhere; she saw no point in leaving her comfort zone. In the course of her life she'd worn several hats – that of precocious teenager, junkie, postal clerk and bartender – in that order. It was the cornucopia of her hard Capricornian edge that had saved from falling through the cracks and down into the druggie underworld. She'd never been timid about her sexuality, having engaged in binges of promiscuity that were conversely followed by weeks, or even months, of an abstinence that would rival that of a nun. She tried to be satisfied with what she had; she'd learned how to be *grateful* in Pal-Anon. She'd observed over the years that rich people tended to be angry and so she came to this conclusion: *Why bother striving? I don't need possessions. Swimming pools, fancy cars and diamonds will never make me happy* ..... That being said, she bought Scratch-Offs regularly, because maybe she was wrong -- and the grass really was greener on the other side?

Pavlina had always been fascinated by the occult. In fact, her favorite tarot card was *La Mort* [although she didn't understand it, she admired the Old World romanticism of the French language and preferred her deck to be *en français*]. *Death is change* ..... *it's transformation* ..... *it's metamorphosis* ..... *and I ain't talkin bout no after life* ..... *I can use this game plan in the here and now*..... she often reminded herself. She was someone who was just trying to get by, to get through, to survive. There were moments when she felt compelled to slip on the rose-colored glasses, but not for too long, for fear that her hunger for kaleidoscopic fantasy would lead her back into the womb of her ninth circle opium den .....

She was heading back to her one-bedroom upper on Foul-Mouth Street between Pencil-Vain-Ya and Joisey. A man in a 1975 Buick Regal pulled over to the curb just as Pavlina was walking by the Palin Street Software Café, two doors down from the Bally-Would Farms bodega. She must have known this man, because she stepped into the front seat just after he'd opened the car door for her. He turned the Buick around at the junction of Woolworth and Palin, drove east on Palin and then made a right turn southward onto Elf-Would Avenue. The two of them continued on to the outskirts of Mucha Nieve, going east on Route 190, then turning to the right and onto Route 90 West, then veering off to the right again to continue southward on Route 219 for about fifteen more minutes. They then exited to the right, and at the end of the ramp, turned right once again onto Alternate Route 20. Three minutes later they reached the hamlet of Porsche Park. The driver turned right onto 240 South and told Pavlina that he needed to get some gas. He pulled into the self-service station right next to Tiny Tim Whore-Ton's. Pavlina used this opportunity to buy some Oldports. Upon entering the shop, to the right of the checkout counter was a dark, seemingly abandoned side room that stretched over to the windowless west-facing wall of the store [it was cheerful in a *Blair Bitch Project* kind of way]. At the southwest corner of this room was an open door, leading to the manager's wood-paneled office; the dull fluorescent overhead light from that office fell across the darkened side room ..... After making her purchase and taking her change from the cashier, who was checking her Dumbphone during the entire transaction and never even made eye contact with Pavlina..... a force beyond Pavlina's comprehension started to pull her towards the doorway to the manager's office ..... *She was being summoned in the same way that Sleeping Beauty had been drawn to the upper rooms of King Stefan's castle by Maleficent ..... to prick her finger on the spindle* ..... On the manager's desk was the Porn Key, a twenty-four ounce can of LaFrack's Brew, by means of which she could physioanimate to her next destination – that being the mansion of Koontessa Klarissa Koontberger. The manager must have just stepped out because the books he'd been reviewing were open and a cigarette was still burning in a red ceramic ashtray [it was his office and he could smoke in it if he wanted to]. The can of LaFrack's Brew was open and half empty. Pavlina reached out and picked up the partially filled can without even looking at it. She entered the nearby bathroom and opened the small frosted glass window that led to the back parking lot. She was then pulled through that window as if she was going through a wormhole ..... the next thing that she knew, she found herself on the third floor landing of the Koontberger manor, right next to the Shrine to Bast .....

KOONTESSA
KLARISSA KOONTBERGER

Koontessa Klarissa Koontberger and her part-
ner Glorie-Whole Evil-Lynne Koontberger (née
Gigglefoock) were an aristocratic lesbian couple that lived in a spacious yet creepy mansion,
The Crew-Ella de Parkay Villa, in Douchebag,
Nueva Jork in the western Cats-Kills. The Crew-
Ella de Parkay Villa was a Vicktorian style manor
surrounded by a landscaped estate, featuring a
mile-long ass-fault driveway that ran through the
center of an immaculate green lawn. This paved
and private road sloped gently upward as one
proceeded towards the mansion. The stretch of
land directly in front of the manor featured statues and pathways enclosed within a French gar-
den, its design having been inspired by *L'année*

dernière à Marienbad[24]. The Koontbergers had two adopted children, of indeterminate sexuality, named Froompie and Kroonchie. But those two children were just for show. There were actually two other young ones – *the family secret* – who'd been born to Glorie-Whole by means of artificial insemination ..... the first being a daughter named Pootsie, who lived in the attic in less than favorable conditions. With her black hair strewn in her face, she resembled Samara, the ghostly young girl from *The Ring*[25]. In the attic, Pootsie played with her rag dolls and appeared to be unaware of the dire nature of her circumstances. When her parents dressed her up for one of their extravagant parties and then brought her downstairs to be presented to skeptical guests ..... she spoke only when spoken to, and then only in a rough whisper. She did, however, possess a special gift. If anyone visiting happened to offend Pootsie during her brief hiatus from seclusion ..... she would shoot potent beams of green fire out of her eyes, incinerating her targets. Her manifestation of this particular ability was no coincidence, as she was in fact ..... *The Doppelgänger of The Lost Child of ..... The Village of The Damned*[26]. The second family secret was a son by the name of Fezziwig Fauntleroy, who was imprisoned in a basement room of The Crew-Ella de Parkay Villa. He idolized *The Ghost of Christmas Yet To Come* and dreamt of being in the employ of Ebenezer Scrooge and Jacob Marley – so that he could become a clerk, rub his hands together in drafty workspaces, buy a coal scuttle and keep the accounts by nineteenth century candle light ..... In her attic prison, Pootsie worshipped The Ghost of Marion Rolf, as portrayed by Karen Black in *Burnt Offerings*[27]. In the cellar where Fezziwig Fauntleroy was kept captive, he paid homage to yet another one of his idols, The Cowboy from *Mulholland Drive*[28]. In that dungeon, there was a secret tunnel leading to the modest 1960s era bungalow of the Koontberger's nearest neighbors, the Kisschrist family [the parents had gotten the house for a steal, since the front yard looked out onto heavily traveled Interstate 77]. The Kisschrist's eldest daughter, Charlene Chiffarobe Kisschrist, insisted on sitting in a rocking chair in front of the large rectangular living room window of the bungalow, where she performed an ongoing impersonation of Mrs. Allerdyce [also portrayed by Karen Black in *Burnt Offerings*]. Sometimes Charlene would even stay up for the entire night, with all of the lights blazing, staring out of the living room window and listening to the *whoosh* of the traffic passing by on Route 77 .....

GLORIE-WHOLE "GIGI" EVIL-LYNNE GIGGLEFOOCK-KOONTBERGER

At first Glorie-Whole had tried to be with men. Because that was what she thought she'd wanted. But after years as a practicing heterosexual; after a string of damaging experiences – she'd decided that men were pigs. Not only did she consider them to be *Schweine* – she also believed that they were in love with the idea of being pigs. And that was when she turned to women. Something that she'd thought she'd never do. Gigi believed -- at least in the context of a committed relationship -- that women were more giving, more caring, more intuitive, more compassionate. But after having lived with Klarissa Koontberger for seven years – Glorie-Whole had decided that Klarissa was just another *Seven Year Bitch*. Thus embittered, she merely tolerated her current situation ..... Not only had Gigi been a bisexual, she'd briefly encountered fame as a porn star in her youth. Once that episode of her life had ended – Gigi had been fortunate enough to legitimize herself by marrying her sugar mama Klarissa.

Certainly no one that Gigi had known while she'd been making skin flicks had ever been uptight about their sexuality. On the other hand, to deal with the commercialization of such a basic instinct ..... one had to be emotionally disconnected. For the sake of their sanity, these *pornographique* actors followed Eros ..... and not Thanatos [though Thanatos would eventually come to greet some of them prematurely, whether they desired to make his acquaintance or not]. These *back in the day* porn stars carried no baggage, they felt the weight of no ball and chain ..... and this had served them well. They'd been right to be pleasure seekers; they'd been right to experience life as a carnal feast. Because if it ended up that sexual connection was the only true connection – then that was better than not having connected at all .....

What Gigi didn't know was that everything that was happening to her had been preordained by the Universe and its agent Maya Hiyuh Powuh, who'd placed a spell upon her, forcing her to reflect upon her dishonorable past – until she'd reached a state of Buddhistic detachment. At which time she could then rejoin the actual and material worlds with the benefit of an advanced awareness, as well as with a new sense of control over her compulsive desires ..... Maya Hiyuh Powuh banished Gigi to *The Would Between the Whirlds* -- a peaceful environment comprised of black and white birch trees, chartreuse green grass, sky blue pools and clear bubbling brooks. In the nighttime of *The Would Between the Whirlds*, white-hot stars shimmered against an indigo firmament. It was a Walt Disney *Sleeping Beauty* "Briar

Rose" kind of refuge ..... calm and mellow ..... clear and serene. It was just too good to be true – and so what was the catch? When would Maleficent emerge from behind her wall of thorns and transform herself into a dragon? When would all of this tranquility explode into a violent, angry orgy of volcanic red orange yellow and the smoky gray purple black of annihilation? From the Olympian heights of her Third Eye Mind Koont Violet Shock-Ra Power Base, Maya Hiyuh Powuh conveyed the following message to Glorie-Whole .....

..... *It is time to develop the conscience that you never had, to bring to light all of the projects that you've sabotaged, and to truly know the men or women that you could have fully loved, had you not feared your own capability for intimacy. All of your soulless libidinal encounters, all of the times that you got fucked in your search for satisfaction ..... did it amount to anything beyond a cheap thrill ..... if you were lucky enough to even experience that? Your pornographique career was a way*

*for you to escape from your all-encompassing
loneliness, it had nothing to do with love, if love
even exists ..... Does love exist, Gigi Gigglefoock? Tell me what you know, you Chock Full
of Anti-Shock-Ra Goddess! ..... don't slip away
into the disillusionment of Dori-Anna Gray! Tell
me that love exists! ..... if you say that this is so
..... I'll believe you .....*

Since she'd left her life of ill repute behind her,
Gigi had had to learn how to think ..... how to focus
on concepts and ideas. She found this to be a challenge, due to the fact that as a child, she'd been
abused by her father -- who'd convinced her at an
early age that she was an idiot. Her dad had been
no genius himself; he just tore her down to make
himself feel important in his armchair-pseudo-intel-
lectual world. He'd read the evening news in the
living room -- after yet another hard day of middle
management paper pushing fund raising .....

Gigi was now committed to becoming an amal-
gam of Saint Francis and Saint Augustine ..... to
metamorphose into a female version of the com-

bined essence of those two saints. Glorie-Whole had lost interest in pursuing actual sex; as needed, she was content to make use of Internet *pornographie* as her sole sexual outlet. *The Would Between the Whirlds* was a perfect metaphor for her current state of being. She'd accepted the idea that she was sexually ambiguous, even sexually confused ..... and perhaps ultimately asexual? That last idea scared her. Something about letting go of one of the most fundamental human urges seemed to be just plain wrong. Thus she was afraid of what other people would think about her if they were to find out ...... who and what she really was. Would they think she'd become a *nun*? What an outdated judgment! She didn't need an excuse to be asexual ..... The real reason for her current sexually indeterminate state was this: she'd never understood the relationship between love, sex and affection. She would now turn to Maya Hiyuh Powuh to find a new and better way to fulfill her life .....

PAVLINA PERESTROIKA AND THE POWDER BLUE BLANKET

..... Now finding herself on the third floor landing of the Koontessa Klarissa Koontberger mansion,
right next to the Shrine to Bast, Pavlina proceeded
to her left, towards the doorway at the end of the
hallway. Once inside, her gaze fell upon a baby
asleep in its crib next to the side window of this elegant bedroom. She approached the baby and
then placed it in a powder blue blanket that was
neatly folded on top of a chest of drawers beside
the crib. She then held up the blanket like a sack.
The infant started yowling and Pavlina was beset
by panic; but then the baby inexplicably calmed
down. Still under the spell of the mysterious force
..... Pavlina retraced her steps back to the Shrine to

Bast, where she and the baby then disappeared by means of Porn Key [LaFrack's Brew] physioanimation ..... reappearing in the bathroom of the gloomy, fluorescently lit manager's office in Tiny Tim Whore-Ton's in Porsche Park, Nueva Jork. She walked out of the office and passed through the darkened side room. She exited Tiny Tim Whore-Ton's and stepped back into the 1975 Buick Regal. She and the driver turned left onto 240 North, shortly thereafter making a left onto Alternate Route 20, driving to the outskirts of the village of Porsche Park and then making a right onto 219 North. Twenty minutes later, after reaching the eastern border of Mucha Nieve, they veered onto the right side exit for 190 West that took them to Miasma Falls. They continued on until they reached the Reign-Beau Flag Bridge that crossed over into Fart Eerie, Bomb-Scary-O, Kanuckya. The driver pulled over to the curb. Pavlina stepped out of the car and then strode onto the overpass with the infant in a blanket. Curiously, no one stopped her in this nether zone between two countries. When she'd reached the halfway point on the bridge, she raised the sack over the pedestrian railing and released the baby, letting it fall into the swirling waters of the Miasma River gorge. The infant screamed during its descent and then there was silence. Pavlina started walking back towards the Amourrica Profundan side of the overpass. But just before she reached that side, she froze cat-like in her tracks ..... *Was Maleficent calling her again?* She turned around and walked back towards the Kanuckyan side of the bridge. Just before getting to the Kanuckyan side, she hesitated once again. She pivoted around, this time proceeding more deliberately. She arrived back at the spot where she'd dropped the baby from the overpass. She climbed over the pedestrian railing and did a swan dive off of the overpass, gliding gracefully into the river .....

BACK IN PALIN-TOWN

..... Pavlina snapped out of her trance. She was standing stock still in front of the Palin Street Software Café. The driver of the 1975 Buick Regal was still waiting by the curb with the engine running and the door open. She stepped inside the car. The driver was her friend – Bobby Bluetooth, a former comedian who'd dropped out the business years ago -- but who still performed from time to time when things got slow at his job as a real estate broker. He'd just finished performing his latest *tight twenty* – his current *killer set* – as the opening act at a place across the street called Café Nibelheim [named after Friedrich Nibelheim, an iconoclastic Doucheylander who in the late nineteenth century had authored a provocative, controversial and philosophical work entitled *How To Roast An Aura*]. Bobby was the one guy Pavlina could trust of all the men that she'd ever known. He wasn't great looking and he wasn't even particularly entertaining. But when Pavlina needed to vent ..... he listened. Bobby's act was lowest common denominator; he felt no need to take intellectual risks. Audiences tended to be difficult and unpredictable enough as it was ..... so he was better off playing it safe .....

BOBBY BLUETOOTH
ROCKS THE MIKE

(Bobby steps out from behind the red velvet curtain and into the center stage spotlight) How's everybody doin tonight? How ya feelin? Is everybody havin a good time? EXCUSE ME I CAN'T HEAR YOU *(crowd screams back various responses like "make us laugh", "keep your day job", "go fuck your mother")*. That's more like it! You did a very good impression of animals at the zoo! *(audience is silent)*. Is anyone here from Joisey? I'll speak slower *(Bobby repeats "I'll speak slower" into the microphone in a Satan voice – scattered laughter)*. I'm Bobby Bluetooth, and I play clubs and colleges up and down the Eastern seaboard. Excuse me one second *(he pulls out his Dumbphone)* ..... just checkin to see if anyone sexted me *(waitress drops a tray of glasses; everyone cheers)*. Let's keep it goin for our waitress, the lovely and talented Chiselina! Chiselina's workin hard for you tonight. Chiselina's husband is a fireman, and whenever

they spend some spare time together, they enjoy pole dancin. KEEPER? (crowd alternately boos and laughs). And let's keep it goin for our emcee, Johnny Banali. Funny guy – right? They don't make 'em like that anymore. (Bobby yells through the curtain to backstage) Hey Johnny, your mother loves you! (Johnny yells back: Go fuck yourself Bobby! – everyone laughs). And let's keep it goin for me. Okay? LET'S KEEP IT GOIN FOR ME, LET'S KEEP IT GOIN FOR ME, LET'S KEEP IT GOIN FOR ME! (audience is silent) .....

So how bout we try and get to know one another. Is anybody datin? (no reaction from audience) Is anyone in therapy? (crowd is silent). I've been in therapy for twenty-seven years, and guess what? I'm not gettin any bet-ter ..... I'm still fucked up ..... what can I say? Therapy keeps me off the streets. My therapist is my babysitter ..... (guy in audience imitates a crying baby and everyone laughs). And now on an entirely different note ..... Is anyone here a convicted felon? Does anybody have some crystal meth? Does anyone have some *rock*? I wanna party! Hey – let's all go over to my place after the show and play Twister in olive oil! (*dead silence in audience*). THAT WAS MY CLOSER (*scattered laughter from crowd*) ….. Okay I'll wrap it up now. I'm doin a short set tonight. I paid for my stage time, I rented the club, I worked something out with the management ahead of time. This is my vanity showcase, literally and figuratively. This is the part where fact meets fiction (*audience erupts into sustained, hysterical belly laughs*) …..

One couldn't imagine the show getting any worse than it was already. But that was indeed going to happen. Soon The Jet Set Open Mikers would arrive. The Jet Set Open Mikers flew first class to open mikes and poetry readings around the world: Umsterdumb, Vienna, Paris and Tokyo. They were notoriously bad performers; they indulged heavily on those international flights; they drank too much champagne; they stuffed their faces in the business-class lounges of the Copenhagen, Hamburg and

Zurich airports. Wherever they ended up -- they were always completely incapacitated. Still -- a small sliver of the work ethic of their forebears shone through, pushing them to maintain their commitments, to show up -- no matter how wrecked they were. Most of the time they had to be carried, by their handlers, on stretchers into the venues of their choosing, to which they were granted immediate access, as the management and staff were always bribed ahead of time .....

Once onstage at Café Nibelheim -- The Jet Set Open Mikers would babble on incoherently, spouting misinformation about obscure references, infuriating the audience, and even sympathizing with the spectators for hating them. The depth of The Jet Set Open Mikers' self-hatred was that great; they tried to convert their low-self-esteem into self-deprecating humor ..... but that never worked. The crowds, forced to contend with this slumming Euro trash, had to be contained behind chain-link fences. They inevitably became violent and ended up hurling bottles, tumblers and shot glasses towards the stage. In fact, whenever they toured in Amourrica Profunda -- The

Jet Set Open Mikers would only perform behind a chain-link fence; this demand was clearly stipulated within their contract. Class-warfare-based eruptions of this nature were occurring with ever-increasing frequency in the bars and nightclubs of bankrupt and burnt-out post-industrial Amourrica Profundan cities .....

REMINISCENCES FROM A HILLBILLY CLAIRVOYANT

I were baptized as *Hepzibah Huckleberry* but everone roun here know me as *The Boy Name Uh Bobby-Sue*. Here I sit on the porch of my ole Kentucky home in a state of plainly affable senility. As the mist gathers in this here twilight, I'll leave aside all notions of fancy speakin an say this ..... Thar's a chill up in them thar hills! I can hear them hunters shootin deers! Thems got they orange hunter jackets on and thems right purty colors! I ain't rightly know what kinda guns they be usin. Ain't my specialty. All I know is that them guns is legal and if them wants to rise up against they Big Govern-Meant that supplies all of they benefits them relies on – well then them can jes go ahead and do that if they likes! I'll be jes fine where I am, Big Govern-Meant or no, cuz I built myself a survivalist nukyuhlur fallout shelter in my back yard ..... Even if them dark times is nigh, for now I ken enjoy the quiet life and by that I mean goin to church to sing purty Holie Ghostie songs every Sunday. Sometimes I even bring along my banjo and everone joins in and sings along with one of my favorite hymns -- *Core-Ann Burnin Laidie* [it's the story of a laidie from *another Middle-Eastern-based Abrahamick religion* that didn't know her proper place with regards to the menfolk of her antique time and were executed as an adulteress during them Crusades] ..... There be a light that's shinin down upon all of us that's singin! All usns is forever blessed – and that ain't no bullshit! My pipples in the Church of Hoorny Boore as I call it – that congregation's my Kommune-Needie! Jes as long as you know that when I say *Kommune-Needie* – that ain't to be confused wit no *Kommune-Izm*. Ever one uh my pipples pulled theyselves up by they bootstraps! Them warn't never no Twerkie Shirkies! Warn't no Reds! Warn't no Socialists! Warn't no

Drop Out Drop Acid Hippies! And keep them sex-lovin Oi-Ropeans with they nude beaches and topless bikinis outta these here hills! The Russians are comin ..... The Soviet Bolsheviks are comin ..... Pol Pot's comin to potty train us! And when them do get over here – we'll be ready. My friends with they guns and they right purty colored orange hunter jackets got them an army assembled! Them'll be prowlin around up in them thar hills with they antler hats on ..... Now lissy here: It ain't bad to think youse better than other pipples! Here's a story bout some Gooders huntin down some Badders [I could say them are Aryans or White Suprematists and you'd know what I'd be implyin by that. But it cuts both ways ..... racism is universal and thems that's red, brown, black and yellow are guilty of it as well] .....

Once there were a Yankee girl who come from the city of Mucha Nieve (why the hell an Amourrica Profundan city got itself a Spanishy soundin name – ah sher as hell don't know! Yo no sé!) ..... This here Yankee laidie done killed her baby. Her were a freaky kinda bartender wench that twerked in the night with strippers and drug dealers; her were probably covered with tattoos jes like everone else these days. Well this girl decided that her liked to party and live the high life of a Scarlet Neely O'Hara Letter type of Krack-Hoore – instead uh jes stayin home and bein a Mommer. When the members of my congregation got wind of this situation by means of their Third-Eye Puritanickal Telepathie – them decided that them would take a bus up North and hunt down this Baby Killin Laidie in the name of Lord Jah-Hee-Zeus. Cuz them was all cooped up from bein Hoorny Boores and them jes wanted to have some fun! And so one fine full Moonie night, them traveled to the town of Douchebag, Nueva Jork, in the western Cats-Kills where the Baby Killer was livin, getting around like she done [her had a Russiany kind of name that sounded right Kommunistick]. Them found her out beyond the edge of the village limits, in a clearin in the pines, lyin on her back on a long flat rock, surrounded by a Ring of Fire that protected this Baby Killin Laidie from anyone except them that knew how to break the spell of that powerful enchantment. My good pipples done transformed theyselves into a vengeful mob – which were real good fun the way I see it! Some of them even wore hockey masks and other kinda scary face coverin contraptions that them had seen in horror movies on digital cable TV (although them shoulda been readin they Good Books instead!). The crowd started to dance roun the Baby Killer – shoutin, swearin and singin Holie Ghostie songs that sounded right Satanick – probably cuz a lot of them had trouble stayin on key! Them addressed the Baby Killin Laidie like this ..... "We got our eagle eyes on you – Baby Killer! There's an express train to hellfire and brimstone waitin fer you! And we ain't talkin bout no kinda Polar Express![29] More like the Midnight Express![30] ..... And then because there warn't no water nearby, the wrathful mob started to pray fer rain, to put out the Ring of Fire that would gain them access to the Baby Killin Laidie. But the rain them prayed fer were not what them had expected. Instead of rainin water – It started rainin men! ..... Jes like that faggoty disco song ..... "It's Rainin Men, It's Rainin Men!" that come from the days in the beginnin of the homosexual plague ..... The mob shouted in fear and terror because the men that rained down upon them warn't no kind of Evilangelist-cursed circuit party porno star hunks ..... them were jes dead zombie-like male specimens that had passed on due to the pansy pestilence ..... that's right them had died of the AIDSiez. And so many of them mens fell upon my congregation that them were trapped and suffocated by all of them rigomortified corpses. It were as if all of them had been mowed down by a stampede. Ever last one of my fellow parishioners died – jes on account of them wantin to hunt down a Baby Killer and bring her to vigilante justice! ..... A disturbin silence settled down on the place. Like a fearsome hush that come about right before a twister. The scene resembled one of them kinda Kommunistick gulagish pogroms with its piles of cadavers -- or even like that Jim Jones Jonestown Massacre! Then after all that ..... the heavens finally rained down real rain. It rained in sheets and the Ring of Fire were extinguished in no time at all .....

Then the Baby-Killin Laidie woke up and took in what was going on. Her felt an unspeakable terror and got up and started to run. Her didn't even know where her were – but her knew her were skeered and her wanted to get to higher ground. Because the torrent went on – it were one of them end of the world kinda rains where the water rises up as high as a Folly-Would Revelations movie tsunami wave. And then jes like that the Baby Killer were bein carried away by powerful currents in the freezin cold water with a gray-black night sky in the background. The Baby-Killin Laidie were sucked down into a whirlpool where her were annihilated ….. And so in the end it were Nature – "She Who Wins All Battles" – who once again had her way with the Blue Green Planet.

THE MARIE VERSAILLES TRAILER PARK

Pavlina Perestroika hadn't expired in the Miasma River gorge after all – and neither had the Blue Blanket Baby that she'd dropped off the side of the

Reign-Beau Flag Bridge. Because, unbeknownst to her, the infant itself was a Porn Key. And so Pavlina had also physioanimated after her dive off of the overpass – by virtue of having made physical contact with the baby. Before the infant hit the surface of the Miasma River, it had physioanimated to a highway truck stop rest area nearby the Marie Versailles Trailer Park outside of Oma-Pa, Nebulaska, Fartland, Amourrica Profunda. The baby reappeared on top of a covered toilet seat inside a stall in the men's bathroom of the rest area. A moment later, Pavlina physioanimated into that same enclosure and retrieved the infant. It became immediately apparent to her that a man, in the stall next to her, was engaged in a sexual tryst with another male. *Men are pigs ..... no matter what their sexual orientation* ..... she muttered to herself. All at once, Pavlina heard instructions from the voice of Bast, who spoke like a purring cat, echoing inside her head: *Proceed to the Marie Versailles Trailer Park* ..... Bast chanted over and over ..... Once the two men had finished and were leaving -- Pavlina ran after them. One of the guys was a trucker and she asked him for a ride to the Marie Versailles Trailer Park. A few minutes later the trucker, Pavlina and the baby drove off .....

In the Marie Versailles Trailer Park, Trailer Number Nine led to a *Dead Zone*[31] within *The Twilight Zone*[32]. At the entrance to this mobile home, one was greeted by Nancy Néant -- a cross between Marabel Morgan and circa 1974 Betty Crocker. Nancy was a shellacked platinum blonde who applied her waterproof mascara and frosted blue eye shadow heavily. She stood outside the front door of the trailer, greeting passersby with the kind of smile that was so phony that only children younger than the age of eight could see through it. She offered her visitors pink lemonade [in the wintertime she served them hot cocoa]. She seduced them like a female *Willy Wonka*[33] ..... inferring, by means of her welcoming manner, that she would lead them to *Candyland* ..... when she was in fact the tangibly manifested *Siren of Eros Thanatos*. Those who accepted Nancy's invitation ..... stepped through the doorway of Trailer Number Nine and encoun-

tered The Void, Nothingness, Non-Existence .....
the Inescapable Event Horizon leading to the Nadir
of the Singularity of a Physical and Spiritual Black Hole.
The minute the unfortunate ones stepped over the
threshold of the entrance to Trailer Number Nine –
they were instantly metamorphosed into whatever it was that comprised Nothingness.   And
since they'd become Nothing[34] – they weren't
able to be aware of Anything. They possessed the
conscience and consciousness of stone. As they
didn't exist -- they knew nothing of Non-Existence.
They were devoid of any knowledge of Being
in The Void. Because it wasn't good enough to
just die anymore.   Although Pavlina had been
unaware of it on a conscious level, she'd actually
wanted to dematerialize into Nothingness ..... to
sacrifice even her soul. How poetic it would be
to say that her stardust remains had been reincarnated somewhere within a parallel multiverse. But
there were no stardust remains and there was no
parallel multiverse. There was only The Void .....

FAKEBOOK GIRL
WANTS TO FAKE YOU UP

Hi! How's it going? Did you look at my Fakebook page recently? Did you read any of my posts? Did you read that post of mine – the one where I try to make you feel sorry for me – because I think everyone on Fakebook is ignoring my posts? Are you entertaining somber thoughts again? Are you letting them cloud up your existence? Are you gazing into the dark mirror? Well stop it – just stop it! Start doing your affirmations! Start being mindful! Start meditating ….. Are any of you familiar with the work of Shock-Tea-Party Mundane? Her premise is simple and classic: Picture what you want and it will materialize for you! Anyone can do it; you don't have to be some kind of Che Mary Kay Foul-Thing / Higher Parterre Witch to practice this! Shock-Tea-

Party's work has helped me so much! Self-help books are the only books that I read now. Because as you may have guessed by this point ..... sometimes I get very down. To the point where I can't leave the house to face anyone or anything! Nonetheless – I eventually force myself to go out. I heed the call of The Rebel Within and I dress in beatnik black. This look protects me, like a talisman, from the undue influence of the projections of my borderline personality – that always boomerang back to me! Before I go outside, I like to gaze into the mirror and speak some Doucheylandish:

"Spieglein, Spieglein / An der Wand / Wer ist die Schönste / Im ganzen Land?"
["Mirror, mirror / On the wall / Who's the fairest / Of them all?"]

And then I go to my favorite bookstore, *Shock-Ra Seven.* I charge in there like some punk rocker who's defying the doorman in old school circa 1981 Puta Jork, Nueva Jork [like I used to do with that Outer Bore-Ho doorman, Johnny Banali, when I was bone thin, wearing black eyeliner and painting my fingernails black]. And then I proceed to the self-help aisle, my equivalent of paradise, to peruse titles that speak to my condition ..... *How to Make Frienemies and Alien-Hate People, The Road Morewhore Traveled, Unfollow Your Diss* – and finally *The Astonishing Repercussions of the Not-So-New-Age Dis-Harmonic Anti-Convergence*. These seminal works have shaped my character ..... Do you have people in your life who are trying to hinder you from making contact with the light? Do you want to let them go – to release them? Then here's what I'd suggest: Banish all that haunts you, all that disturbs you, from your mind! Disperse your dark thoughts and visualize yourself moving towards the light! Use affirmations, meditation, mindfulness! And I don't care how misanthropic you think you are – we're all in this together! Three cheers for secular humanism!

..... This is a momentous occasion. Are you ready? We have arrived at the moment of truth: I am not of your world! *I am Agnosticka -- Ruler of the Nine Known Multiverses!* Although I am an alien -- albeit one in humanoid female form -- we have so much in common! I am still your Best Fiend Forever! I will always be your Favorite Frienemy! And to prove this to you, I will now sing the praises of Fakebook ..... *Oh Fakebook! You are my Hello Kitty Snuggle Bunny! When I step into the Land of Fakebook -- I am immediately awash in hugs, tickles, giggles, rainbows, sweetness, warm fuzzies, pastel sea foam mist, jazzy golden tears, pink and blue cupcakes and twilight walks in green summer parks ..... Oh Fakebook! You are that rare moment of my childhood that offered me solace ..... You are my Saturday morning hell-ementary school arts and crafts course where I made projects with glitter and glue ..... You are my grandmother's ramshackle blue-gray Cape Cod summer house surrounded by a sand dune jungle ..... You are the cupola-covered bandstand of the village green; a place where everyone gathers to support each other; a place where everyone receives positive valida-tion ..... Oh Fakebook! You are like an Amourrica Profundan homogeneous breeder suburb that attempts unsuccessfully to shelter its inhabitants from the geopolitical horrors of the Blue Green Planet Small World Global Village Nightmare .....*

GIOVANNI ZSAZSASKY GOES TO VULTURE

Giovanni Zsazsasky used to patronize a bar called Vulture that was located at the corner of Eleventh Avenue and West Twenty-Second Street, Puta Jork, Nueva Jork, Amourrica Profunda. In major megalopopolitan areas of the Western World on the Blue Green Planet, during the time before Reign-Beau Flags had exposed the pre-viously secret society of gay men – *Vulture* bars had grown into a franchise that catered to the leather-rubber-fetish lifestyle. At the Puta Jork Vulture -- Giovanni could usually find what he was looking for. Men who were "casual", "looking for fun", "live and let live". A scenario so typical of queer men in Puta Jork; one that comprised promiscuity, dalliances, one-night stands ..... relationships between two men that were referred to as friendships, when in fact the two males in question had nothing in common except their respective biological urges .....

In the long run, Giovanni was living a Catch-22. To escape his non-monogamous lifestyle -- he'd need to find someone who only wanted to be with him. But to find that guy -- he'd have to frequent someplace else besides Vulture. Something that he ultimately wasn't willing to do. Giovanni was forever deconstructing every possible instance of perceived rejection that he encountered at the bar. The effects of Vulture had turned his life into a nightmare ..... over the years he'd become increasingly angry, bitter and disillusioned. He managed to keep his head above water, but the damage was starting to show. He became less interested in forming and maintaining friendships with gay men ..... as the chasm of misunderstanding between himself and most of his queer brothers continued to widen. And so he developed a taste for objectifying male specimens in sex clubs, dark rooms and bathhouses. He'd learned nothing about intimacy during his thirty-year experiment with decadent nightlife. Besides -- there were better places in which to practice hedonism than in Puta Jork. He'd started traveling to Brrrlin, Doucheyland, Oi-Ropa and ended up experiencing a similar fetish scene there -- albeit one that was noticeably less shaming than was the case in Puritanickal Amourrica Profunda. In Brrrlin, a different attitude existed towards sexuality; particularly with regard to gay male sexuality. The cultural differences were subtle -- yet palpable .....

KRISTOFER PETROGRAD-FALKLAND

Kristofer Petrograd-Falkland came from Pearl Jamington, Fartmont, Amourrica Profunda, where he'd been traumatized during his upbringing. And so he vowed to never return to that place. As soon as he'd graduated from Half Crack Pipe High School, he took off for what was then the center of Amourrica Profundan decadence; that hotbed of creativity that was known as Puta Jork, Nueva Jork. In brief -- he fell in with the wrong crowd of queer men.   They weren't advancing in their careers; they weren't striving for something better; they weren't giving. They were taking ..... As if it wasn't difficult enough dealing with those kind of hustlers – Kristofer had a secret that weighed on him heavily. He was sexually confused, sexually ambiguous, sexually ambivalent, sexually indeterminate – and he often felt asexual. Still – he could appear to be the macho hottie if he wanted to and he used this skill to his professional advantage .....

Kristofer became obsessed with a bar called Schmack that was located in the Beast Village, Puta Jork. He'd never been employed in a nine to five job. He was a go go boy who'd recently taken up pole dancing in an effort to expand his options. Once he'd resolved to make a serious commitment to pole dancing, he decided to undergo castration to lessen the crotch friction that he'd encounter in his new career ..... Kristofer started moonlighting at Schmack as a stripper ..... Schmack was a shadowy space, a lurid red-lit hellhole filled with cackling, hostile he-bitches ..... where patrons stuck their heads through the legs of the dancers to purchase drinks. Before he started his shift, Kristofer would shove two rolled-up socks into his jockstrap and then play hard to get as he gyrated on top of the bar. Somehow he got away with this ..... because he usually managed to pick up a haul of cash before the end of the night. He always stayed late after he worked because he didn't want his colleagues to catch a glimpse of his genital mutilation. When Mr. Trini Tripple-XXX, one of the other go go boys, happened to see him naked in the dressing room, and noticed that instead of a cock, he had only a horrible-looking scar – Trini laughed out loud at Kristofer – behavior of this nature being common among the cruel gay alpha males of their profession. Kristofer was so humiliated by the fact that his genital wound had been revealed ..... that he decided to stop time. Somehow Kristofer had acquired the ability to freeze time after seeing the film *Interstellar*[35]. Therefore instead of lashing out with rage -- Kristofer afforded himself a moment to make a decision as to how he would murder Mr. Trini Tripple-XXX. First of all, he didn't want there to be any blood. Secondly, he didn't want to make any direct physical contact with Trini. He'd recently seen a lackluster straight-to-DVD film in which Shannon Doherty whacked a psychopathic security guard on the back of the head with a section of steel pipe. Serendipitously, there happened to be a piece of metal pipe in the Schmack dressing room due to an ongoing renovation. Kristofer grabbed the section of steel pipe, positioned himself behind Trini..... and then started time again. Before Trini had a chance to react, Kristofer whacked him fiercely on the back of his skull. Mr. Trini Tripple-

XXX immediately fell forward; there were no question that he was dead. Kristofer rolled up Trini in a filthy brick red and burnt orange carpet that was stored in the dressing room broom closet. He then dragged the rug and Trini's body outside and hoisted him into the green recycling dumpster that stood at the back of a neighboring parking lot. He went back inside to the dressing room and put the piece of metal pipe back where he'd found it .....

Kristofer had a talent that any human possesses, should they choose to access it. From that point on ..... anyone who put him down, condescended to him, considered him to be stupid or treated him with disrespect ..... would pay the ultimate price. They would regret having been foolish enough to have become Kristofer's friend ..... If they were unlucky enough to even be aware of regret in those final moments before their journey into Nothingness .....

Kristofer Petrograd Falkland was apprehended and arrested shortly thereafter. Three of the Schmack go-go boys, who'd been working on the night that Mr. Trini Tripple-XXX had been murdered, spoke to the police about Kristofer's attitude and strange behavior; they concurred that he was a ticking time bomb. Although he'd left his fingerprints on the section of steel pipe he'd used as a murder weapon ..... during the ensuing investigation, the handling of the evidence was botched due to shoddy police work and ended up being a liability for the prosecution. And so Kristofer was acquitted and went on to enjoy success in a fake-reality show patterned after MSNBC's *Lock Up*. Subsequent spinoffs of Kristofer's show – *Benjy the Articulate Porn Star* and *Dobbie Does Humblewhore* – became successful as well.

Copy for Promotional Spot for Benjy the Articulate Porn Star:

More than a sex machine, Benjy leaves behind his career in the demi-monde of por-

nographie, turning his life around in the manner of a modern-day Saint Francis Augustine, to become a truly no-bull No-Bull Prize-winning author.

Copy for Promotional Spot for Dobbie Does Humblewhore:

The fall from grace of "The Weak-Ed Kwyddytch Bitch of the Third Eye Mind Koont" (inspired by the works of Che Mary-Kay Foul-Thyng).

The tale of the murder, of Kristofer's acquittal and subsequent career success, were eventually made into a film, entitled *The Flickering Tongues of Porn*, directed by the controversial Oi-Ropean director Bars von Bier. Although the account of this homicide, as it had actually occurred, was relatively straightforward as far as murder cases go – Von Bier changed the facts to suit the purposes of his cinematic vision. *The Flickering Tongues of* Porn ended up winning the coveted Napalm War award at the Can't Film Festival in Can't, Frenchyland.

THE HAUNTING OF EBAY

It was a bout of manically tinged insomnia that inspired Giovanni's Zsazsasky's *You-Freaka* moment. He'd recently heard that a reclusive, self-loathing, sexually indeterminate mega rock star was addicted to shopping on EBay. In fact, this pop star spent so much time on the site that he was actually haunting EBay. EBay had come to be known, by the majority of the Amourrica Profundan populace, as a go-to pacifier in moments of thumb-sucking sadness; a necessary evil that helped the user to fill up their emptiness with superfluous goods. Because the beneficial effects of the therapy, the affirmations, the positive thinking, the self-help books and the Twelve Step groups had stopped working. Thus the only choice for the aggrieved victim of *life is not fair* was this: to haunt EBay ..... Once the EBay addict realizes that there's no cure for those endless nights of online shopping -- the only thing left to do is this: ONE MUST GIVE UP EBAY ..... NO MORE HAUNTING EBAY .....

Should you find out that your friend is haunting EBay, then either perform an intervention on their behalf, or declare to them that the friendship is over. Because you want better of them and there won't be any possibility of mutual respect in the relationship until they KICK THE EBAY HABIT ..... until they STOP HAUNTING EBAY ..... until they FIND A SUBSTITUTE CREATIVE OUTLET .....or CHANNEL THEIR PAIN INTO THEIR WORK ..... EVEN DRAG QUEEN BINGO AS A SUBSTITUTE PASTIME WILL BE ACCEPABIBBLE .....

HAIKUS ABOUT EBAY
BY GIOVANNI ZSAZSASKY

HAIKU EB1
Overpower me
Will you take away my time?
Under your control

HAIKU EB2
He haunted EBay

So much he wanted to buy

A window shopper

HAIKU EB3

Drag queens shop EBay

Looking for some flashy pumps

To rock their next show

THE COLLECTIVE WE OF FAGGOTS LIKE US WHO COSTUMED AS A TRAGIC GREEK CHORUS SPEAK TO GIOVANNI ZSAZSASKY DURING HIS REM SLEEP

Don't you wish that you could be LIKE us? We represent *The Collective We of Faggots LIKE Us*. We love LGBTQ pride parades, drag queens with biting tongues, glossy magazines filled with primary colors and articles about nothing in miniscule print ..... We are professional go-go boys. We were paid to be on that Elf-Abba float in the Puta Jork, Nueva Jork Gay Pride Parade! By Stanley Thornside, a sexually confused, tormented and decrepit rich old man with a taste for twinkles [by *old* we mean any non-breeder over fifty who goes to the gym less than three times a week. In that respect – Stanley is *ancient*] ..... As adolescents, we were precocious; we were born to be bold, brave, fearless and at home with our desires. We never had any sexual insecurities. We're so sorry about all of those mainstream homosexuals who have to work nine to five jobs. We're perfectly content being bartenders and coat check boys .....

It's not even that we love what everyone thinks we're supposed to love; that which an out-rageous over-the-top screaming queen should delight in; that which is supposed to be pleas-ing to a conformist follower of the tribe. It's just a coincidence that we love what most people think we should love. We're so lucky that we fit into a politically correct spectrum of queer life that we've never questioned. We love what the state of the art gay world has given us. It makes our time on the planet as faggots so much easier

..... We are not angry, we don't understand irony, we love our female divas. We feel free wherever we are, we enjoy life, we are relaxed, we go on gay cruises, we go to circuit parties, we are tanned and toned, we sport tribal tattoos. We love to dance in the basement of El Monstro, Harridan Square, Puta Jork ..... We are not cold, uncompassionate bitches! Just because we suppress our emotions with hyper-sexuality for the sake of *fun* – doesn't mean that we are not warm and loving as well. If you tell us we are animals – we accept that. We are hot-blooded Rose Red as well as cold-blooded Vulkan Green. We like to wear golden-olive crocodile-cat eye contact lenses, with which we can stun, seduce and paralyze our prey. We are like cobras on mattresses with our flickering tongues of porn; we act like porn stars even if we're not. We love Rio, we love Ibizaah, we love South Bitch, we have sugar daddies. We go where the rich men take us as long as they pay for our hotel and airfare. Designer clothes, interesting personalities, stimulating conversation, breathtaking skylines, fabulous hotels, five star restaurants, even Puta Jork Fraud-Gay shows .....

Before we go -- there's one more thing we'd like to say and that is this: WE'RE COMPLETELY AGAINST GAY SHAME! IN FACT, WE'RE ASHAMED OF ANYONE, OF ANY ORIENTATION, WHO FEELS ANY KIND OF SHAME! WHY BOTHER? LIFE IS TOO SHORT! WHY WASTE YOUR TIME ON THE NEGATIVITY OF SHAME! IF YOU WERE SEXUALLY TRAUMATIZED IN YOUR CHILDHOOD OR YOUTH – JUST GET OVER IT! HERE'S OUR ADVICE: READ A CHAPTER OF AN ANTI-SHAME SELF-HELP BOOK BEFORE YOU GO OUT AND GET LOADED AT THE BAR! OR GO ON LONG WALKS ON THE BEACH – UNDER A FULL MOON IF YOU CAN – AND WALK OFF THE SECRET SHAME! LIFE'S A BITCH FOR EVERYONE – NOT JUST FOR PEOPLE WHO FEEL SHAME! WE'RE ASHAMED TO BE TALKING ABOUT SHAME -- EVEN THOUGH WE DON'T HAVE SHAME. BUT IF WE DID – OUR SHAME OF OUR SHAME WOULD BE OUR SECRET SHAME! WE'RE ASHAMED THAT WE EVEN ADMITTED THIS TO YOU!

THE RAINBOW FLAG BOYS
[IS IT FUN YET?]

Bobby and Tommy both wore rainbow flag-colored suits. And they dressed up their two adopted boys, Seaside and Sunshine, in the same way. They painted their homes on Fire Island and in Provincetown with rainbow flag stripes. And their custom designed jet that flew them between those two locales was adorned with rainbow flag stripes as well. They sported rainbow flag bikinis at the beach, wore rainbow flag contact lenses, had rainbow flag tattoos and drank rainbow-striped margaritas [if the bartender didn't know how to mix rainbow striped margaritas, then they switched colors with each new drink; they progressed from mango to curaçao to pomegranate]. They paid homage to their favorite film, *Prissy Scylla-Charybdis of Desserts*, by going in drag in rainbow flag wigs, gowns, dashikis, bellbottoms and glitter-coated platform shoes. And finally – they defecated rainbows, they evacuated rainbows out of their colons, Mother Nature expelled rainbows out of their asses. Nonetheless – their daily dialogue reflected the essential element of true love that existed within the parameters of their relationship:

Bobby: "I'M SHITTING OUT A FUCKING RAINBOW – TOMMY!"

Tommy: "ME TOO BOBBY! MY COLON NEEDS TO EXPRESS ITS MANIFESTLY MULTI-SPECTRAL NATURE IN A WAY THAT REPRESENTS HARMONIOUS TOLERANCE!"

They were a living, breathing, non-breeder combination of *Sergeant Pepper's Lonely Hearts Club Band* and *The Boys in The Band*. They were politically correct by reason of their being married but other than that – they did as they chose. They listened to the beats of their respective drummers; they travelled roads that were frequented by many, as well as by just a few. They enrolled their boys in pre-kindergarten classes at the Monty-Clift-Sorry school. They lived in fear of the color shit brown. And that's why they kept their assholes very clean. They kept themselves apprised of the latest state-of-the-art enemas. They needed to freshen up their colons on a regular basis. Because they also made hardcore leather porn films – just the two of them. They lived their queer life the way most Amourrica Profundans pictured the life of a cliché homosexual. They were out loud and proud. They didn't care about being brilliant; they didn't care about winning a Hieronymous Boscar; they weren't insecure. Life is what you make it and they were making it *FUN*. They lived for the moment .....

HOW GREEN WAS MY CALDERA

THE GRRRRLS
WHO LOVED WEAK-ED
TOO MUCH

Back in nineteen-eighties Puta Jork, Nueva Jork there was a Howard Johnson's restaurant that stood at the corner of West Forty Sixth Street and Fraud-Gay. Going west a little way from that corner was the Gaiety Male Burlesque Theatre where young bucks stripped onstage for older and, more likely than not, decrepit *gentilshommes d'un certain âge* ..... where chicken hawks would cruise for twinkies. These types of places were common back then in the areas to the west and north of Those Thymes Not-So-Square. In the spirit of Eros, other red light district establishments in the area took their names from certain iconic works of Renaissance sculpture-such as David, Adonis and

Venus. The Gaiety also functioned as an unofficial club for men who had sex with men – be they fags, fruits, queers, queens, pansies, screamers, non-breeders or any other politically-incorrect moniker for *homosexual* – terms like those still widely in use during the height of the AIDS crisis when the fear of contagion and death permeated the core of the gay male community .....

A couple of doors down from the Gaiety was a rehearsal studio that called to mind the lyrics from "At The Ballet" from *A Chorus Line* ..... *Up a steep and very narrow stairway / To the voice like a metronome* ...... One literally ascended such a staircase to get to the rehearsal rooms with out-of-tune upright pianos ..... where triple-threat hopefuls, singers in showcases and even blatant amateurs belted out standards from Fraud-Gay musicals – that they were presumably preparing as audition pieces. All of these locales comprised the seemingly odd -- yet ultimately logical for that time -- juxtaposition of the sacred, the profane, the commercial and the hopeless [the hopeless being *The Wounded of Fraud-Gay* – those who were never cast, yet who never stopped auditioning]. All of these places were jumbled together in the shadows and bleak spaces between the bright lights of the theatres of the Great No-Longer-As-White-Fraud-Gay .....

But by the time the year 2003 had rolled around, *La Gran Manzana Corrupta, AKA The Big Rotten Apple*, had started to show signs of a conspicuous gentrification ..... that would eventually banish most of the punks, freaks, beatniks, hippies, hustlers, artists and Off-Off-Fraud-Gay theatres from Woman-Hattan – to the previously sketchy and / or blatantly provincial neighborhoods of The Outer Bore-Hos. Those who remained *below Fourteenth Street,* particularly in the Beast Village and on the Lower Beast Snide, were essentially marooned. These stalwarts began to complain about how the city had changed. They mourned their dying communities and the disappearance of the so-called avant-garde [even though according to Aloe-Vera Ginseng – the counterculture had ceased to exist in Amourrica Profunda as of 1980]. At the same time these keepers of the flame realized that they'd gotten older and that Woman-Hattan had changed – just as Paris, London and Umsterdumb had evolved to transcend their previous reputations and demographics. It was hard for these survivors to admit that they were being replaced by a new generation of weekend party people – who filled a niche that combined aspects of *bridge and tunnel*, *neo-faux-hipster professional* and *the perennial transplant from the Amourrica Profundan Fartland* – all of whom liked to dress up and frequent the now pricy bars and restaurants that had taken over the increasingly chic, yet monotonous, neighborhoods of downtown Woman-Hattan. During any free weekend moment when they weren't looking down at their technology – these newbies liked to throw up on the sidewalks in–between bars. Whatever they were called, whoever they were and wherever they came from ..... one thing was for certain ..... the Beast Village was dead ..... the Lower Beast Snide was dead. And maybe even *La Gran Manzana Corrupta* was dead – at least in spirit. Ever since

9-11, it had been rumoured among the older generation of downtown that many of the cool, dressed in black, creative innovators and badass artist-Beau-He-Mans had moved to *La Ciudad de México* – a metropolis that was now being touted as the *Nueva Nueva Jork* .....

Meanwhile well above Fourteenth Street – a new group of young female psycho-sycophants had made their presence known on the West Side of Midtown Woman-Hattan. When this particular group of Outer Bore-Ho / Outer Bore-Hos gathered their forces and came into the city, their focus was directed towards one location with laser beam precision – that being none other than the Gersh-Loser Theatre where *Weak-Ed* was playing. *Weak-Ed* was a mediocre musical featuring a couple of big hits – that appeared to have embarked on an interminable run. The Weak-Ed Wring-Wraith-Leader, who referred to herself as *Elfindaah Glindaabaah*, had grown up in the western zone of the state of Nueva Jork where the Beast Coast morphs into the Fartland ..... Elfindaah was the kind of young laidie, who since ninth grade had always managed to snag the lead role in every musical that her high school had produced. She had an insufferably upbeat and annoying temperament; incessantly smiling and laughing, never angry or depressed. She was always on. She was obsessed with musicals; at least those that were well known within a mainstream context. The majority of her peers believed that she would go on to conquer Fraud-Gay. All of this inspired the rebel Goth chicks in her class to plot against her and to torment her with malicious practical jokes. Yet Elfindaah remained undaunted, she was unstoppable and determined to follow her dream. Immediately after her high school graduation, she moved to Puta Jork to start auditioning for Fraud-Gay musicals. Unfortunately, like so many before her who'd wanted to conquer Fraud-Gay ..... things didn't work out as planned. She became discouraged by the continual rejection and began to hate all musicals except for one: Weak-Ed. After several months of depression, firings from waitress jobs and fights with sociopathic roommates --

Elfindaah discovered a new focus; a way in which to channel her frustrations ..... that being the founding of Weak-Ed Fan Clubs nationwide ..... Having been so inspired, the first thing Elfindaah did was to write out the Ten Commandments of the Obsessed Weak-Ed Fan. Only girls between the ages of thirteen and eighteen [inclusive] were eligible to become Obsessed Weak-Ed Fans. Just as Martin Luther had nailed his Ninety-Five Theses to the door of the All Saints Church in Wittenberg, Doucheyland on October 31st, 1517, consequently sparking the Reformation – The Ten Commandments of the Obsessed Weak-Ed Fan were posted on one of the TKTS booths that were located on a concrete island in the middle of Fraud-Gay ..... in a limbo between East and West Forty-Seventh Streets .....

THE TEN COMMANDMENTS OF THE OBSESSED WEAK-ED FAN

Commandment One: All Obsessed *Weak-Ed*-Loving Girls are required to wear green face makeup in the style of antagonist-pro-tagonist Elf-Abba. They may only purchase green makeup manufactured by Been Denial. Any Obsessed *Weak-Ed*-Loving Girl who fails to wear Been Denial Elf-Abba green face makeup will be driven in the *Bus of Punishment* [modeled after the *Fart-Ridge Family* school bus] to the Go-Wannas Canal where she will then be dunked repeatedly like an accused and accursed seventeenth century Salem, Massachusetts witch.

Commandment Two: Saint Patrick's Day will be honored as the highest of high holy days among Obsessed *Weak-Ed*-Loving Girls. Attendance of the Puta Jork, Nueva Jork, Saint Patrick's Day Parade will be compulsory, to facilitate worship of the color green as it appears, or as it is worn, on Saint Patrick's Day. All *Weak-Ed*-Loving Girls will be monitored on Saint Patrick's Day by *The Baroque and Byzantine Hierarchy Created to Oversee the Well-Being of Obsessed Weak-Ed Fans.*

Commandment Three: Beloved icons from the history of Amourrica Profundan popular culture, such as the *Green Ghost*, the *Green Hornet*, the *Incredible Hulk*, the *Sinclair Dinosaur*, or the *Lucky Charms Leprechaun* – will in no way substitute as "Objects to Be Worshipped by *Weak-Ed*-Loving Girls in Place of Elf-Abba".

Commandment Four: Any Obsessed *Weak-Ed*-Loving Girl who becomes overly preoccupied with Elf-Abba, and then in a fit of comparing and despairing, attempts suicide by jumping from the mezzanine of the Gersh-Loser Theatre and into the orchestra seats – will be granted no chance of reincarnation. Instead, upon impact with the orchestra seats -- a magma-filled chasm will crack open underneath the floor of the theatre and the suicidal *Weak-Ed* fan will subsequently be pulled down into the fiery inferno of *Drag Me To Hell*[36].

[Note from the Obsessed *Weak-Ed* Fans Secretary: Unfortunately hypersensitive young women often become overwhelmed during the process of their transformation into full-fledged Obsessed *Weak-Ed* Fans. And by doing so, they are pushed over the edge -- literally and figuratively. Lately, several evening performances of *Weak-Ed* at the Gersh-Loser Theatre have had to be stopped – because young misses who came to the realization that they would never be Elf-Abba – chose to jump from the mezzanine and into the orchestra seats, critically injuring or killing themselves, as well as various audience members. Thus a decision was handed down from The Upper Echelons of the *Weak-Ed* Fans Management, stating that henceforth any of the aforementioned trespassers, who manage to survive their leap from the mezzanine, will be swallowed up by the fiery inferno of *Drag Me To Hell*.]

Commandment Five: The only *Weak-Ed* character that can be hated by an Obsessed *Weak-Ed*-Loving Girl is Doctor Dilettante the Hoorny Boore Goat Teacher. It is, in fact, compulsory to venomously despise Doctor Dilettante. All Obsessed *Weak-Ed*-Loving Girls must vociferously heckle Doctor Dilettante during any performance that they attend. Even if security succeeds in removing the Obsessed *Weak-Ed*-Loving Girls in question from the theatre during this contemptuous display – no disciplinary action, regarding this matter, will be handed down from The Upper Echelons of the *Weak-Ed* Fans Management.

Commandment Six: The only deity that the Obsessed *Weak-Ed*-Loving Girl will be allowed to worship is the Macy's Thanksgiving Day Parade Elf-Abba Balloon -- that on the day of the parade will be suspended from the top of a Fraud-Gay and Forty Seventh Street TKTS Booth. Lord Szczmawg speaks of this in the Buy-Bull. In this regard, His words must be noted with care:

..... *You shall have no other Goddesses but Elf-Abba ..... You shall not make for yourself an idol, or any likeness of what is in heaven above or on the Blue Green Planet beneath or in the water that covers the surface of the Blue Green Planet .....You shall not worship them or serve them; for I, Lord Szczmawg, am a jealous Szczmawg, visiting the iniquity of the fathers upon the children, upon the third and the fourth generations of those who hate Elf-Abba,...*

Commandment Seven: Should any of the Obsessed *Weak-Ed*-Loving Girls choose to congregate on Ninth Avenue between Forty-Second and Forty Ninth Streets, in the Smells Bitchin neighborhood of Woman-Hattan, Puta Jork, Nueva Jork -- no more than seven hundred Obsessed *Weak-Ed*-Loving Girls [or one-hundred girls per block / fifty girls on each side of the avenue] will be allowed to con-gregate for the purpose of any kind of *Weak-Ed*-related protest; an example of this being demonstrations encouraging Puta Jorkers to attend only performances of *Weak-Ed* and to boycott all other plays and musicals that are currently running on Fraud-Gay.

Commandment Eight: All Obsessed *Weak-Ed*-Loving Girls are responsible for the purchase of their tickets, as well as for their travel expenses, to see *Weak-Ed* on Fraud-Gay. The same policy applies to any Amourrica Profundan or Kanuckyan city where they would travel to see a road company performance of *Weak-Ed*.

Commandment Nine: Any Obsessed *Weak-Ed*-Loving Girl who is caught attending any Fraud-Gay show other than *Weak-Ed* – will be promptly physioanimated to the *Logan's Run*[37] Multiverse for immediate *renewal*.

Commandment Ten: If and when any sign of disrespect is shown to Elf-Abba, by any Obsessed *Weak-Ed*–Loving Girl – such fan will be promptly physioanimated to the *Logan's Run* Multiverse for immediate *renewal*.

SHEENA
HORRORSHOW PRINCESS

A couple of my Grrrlfriends, with whom I communicate via Porn Key physioanimation since we
inhabit different multiverses, and who like myself
are "The Derivative Product of Several Ancient
Mythologies" – are Benson & Hedges fund man-
agers. They are aggressive as hell and I love the
shit out of them! All of those lazy dressed in black
neo-beatnik Beau-He-Mans – a dying breed in
both the Beast Village and the Lower Beast Snide
of Puta Jork, Nueva Jork – whine about how the
rents are so damn high. Well here's what I have
to say to that: Stop sucking your thumbs, get out
of your highchairs and get to work – bitches! Life
goes on, cities change! Life is tough for everyone –
not just you! Adapt! Modulate! The sky's the limit for

the crafty entrepreneur – whatever the economic climate may be ..... You don't have the nerve to become a carpetbagger in bad times and take advantage of other people's suffering ..... you don't even have the balls to get up every morning and go to a minimum wage job ..... Hello! The clock is ticking! Create a business plan, devour self-help books [my personal favorite is "The Whorist's Way" by Jewelry Camera-On], do affirmations – and a five thousand dollar per month studio in a luxury Upper Beast Snide high rise will be yours ..... My Benson & Hedges fund manager Grrrlfriends do NOT need any kind of heavy entertainment to burn them out or to make them think too much after a hard day slogging in the trenches of Puta Jork, the financial capital of the Blue Green Planet! Woo hoo! – La Gran Manzana Corrupta! Big Rotten Apple! And as for Kierkegaard's "The Concept of Anxiety"? Thank Goddess that guy is dead! What a Dobbie Does Dull-Ass Downer! Any and all traces of whatever those nineteenth century dead white males were trying to say should be eradicated and paved

over with the joie de vivre of the Reign-Beau Flag
Faggots Foundation For Fun!

My Benson & Hedges fund manager Grrrlfriends
like to schmooze and network in those trendy
expensive bars in downtown Woman-Hattan
that are filled with fascinating "Anal Sex and The
Sh*tty" type extras! Those beautiful people that
you imagine to be hanging out in Lost Angelist or
South Bitch, filming fake-reality shows. Whether
or not it's true [and I for one believe it to be pure
speculation] that they're empty-headed bubble-
heads, with a spray tan or just too much of a tan,
and with nothing to say – it can't be denied that
they're supremely driven to get attention! And if
they want attention, and this becomes their reason
for living, then they will succeed! Because the XXX-
Istentialist always wins! Their genius is manifested by
virtue of their perseverance alone! Even Friedrich
Nibelheim knew that ..... I love "Anal Sex and The
Sh*tty"! People who put that show down are just
jealous ..... okay those "Anal Sex and The Sh*tty"
girls don't ride horses and battle badass "300" type
guys – they could never do that! Don't get me

wrong – I don't have any delusions about being Sheena Horrrorshow Princess! It's a job that I have to show up for! I don't care what I do! I don't have any integrity ….. When I was twenty-three I had a job sweeping floors in a warehouse in Maspeth, Queers, Nueva Jork. And I'd do it all again – just to be employed. Because anything's better than lounging around afternoons watching Hell-In of Goy Degenerate! Anything is preferable to unemployment ….. The only skill I have in life is this: I can fuck my way onto a mediocre television series if I want to! I'm so glad that I have my Iniquity card! I'm so grateful to my Unholie Trinitie – Maya Hiyuh Powuh, Lord Szczmawg and Lord Jah-Hee-Zeus – for that! You'll hear more about it in a speech that I've prepared for the SAG-FAG-HAG awards! I'm a workhorse – even when I'm not on the horse! Not only do I always get back on the horse – I also never put the fucking pen down! I'll die with a pen in my hand! Je Suis Charlie Angel ….. I'm at work on my minimoir as we speak and it will hit the presses and be available wherever books are sold before the end of the fiscal year …..

But shop talk is a bore! My Benson & Hedges fund manager Grrrlfriends prefer the cartoon-esque, graphic novel-inspired films of Thing-Mar Bubblegum, as well as the music of Swing Out Twisted Sister and Amazing Disgrace of Base! That's right – they like elevator music! Which is entirely appropriate because they spend so much time in elevators going back and forth between all of those high-pressure meetings that are the beating heart of their careers! Make no mistake – my Benson & Hedges fund manager Grrrlfriends are the new heroes of Woman-Hattan, Puta Jork, Nueva Jork! They will set the tone for the future. And even though they have MBAs and PhDs ..... They like pretty dresses, designer shoes (like Scary Bad-Snore from "Anal Sex and The Sh*tty") and fan-tastic three-day weekends in Middl Earf Frampton! They've modeled their lives around the fake-reality show, "The Return of Dumbspeak", starring Gym Part-Fascism. They love their work and they love life! They're too busy number crunching to read books! And who can blame them? Books are so over! Don't read books anymore – read Wikipedia! And

*if no one's written a Wikipedia page about you --
I don't want to know you! Go get some credits –
then I'll hang out with you! Even if you only manage to produce a weekly variety show on basic
cable – at least you're trying! Check this out:
When I'm in the mood for something primitive – I
like to text my friends on a non-Internet flip phone
..... I'm Low-Tech! I feel so prehistoric like a Crow-
Fag-Anon or like a Knee-Andro-Gal chick who
keeps the home fires burning in a cave in Gee-
Brawl-Tar! Don't ever underestimate the impor-
tance of Home and Hearth ..... Don't you judge
me! You're no better than me! I'm both "The Girl
Next War" and "The Girl Next Whore"! For Maya-
Hiyuh-Powuh's sake!*

LA
SCHADEN-
FREUDE
DE
JEAN-
NETTE

JEAN-NETTE
THE JET LAG FAG HAG

Jean-Nette the Jet Leg Fag Hag was married, lived in Pornchester, Nueva Jork and resentfully watched over her husband's kids from a previous marriage. So whenever she got the chance to escape from her suburban prison and go out on the [small] town – she'd use that free time to chat with her Grrrlfriends, all of whom were women of achievement. Jean-Nette, however, had rejected the career path, citing her non-competitive nature as the cause. And she was lucky because she had some money. She hadn't had to earn her sophistication; it had been handed to her by virtue of good fortune. She hadn't grown up expecting that she would be financially independent, thus she became conflicted about her fiscal freedom, once she realized that a comfortable lifestyle was within her grasp ..... After Jeanette and The Grrrlfriends had downed a few cosmos and had finished discussing PTA meetings, television shows and the gossip they'd overheard in the supermarket – they moved on to more R rated fare. In this regard, Jean-Nette was more advanced than The Grrrlfriends. After a certain point in the conversation, notably once Jean-Nette realized that she'd pissed off one of the group – she'd talk about how she liked to spend a lot of time on her knees .....

Jean-Nette:

(soliloquy) Well reading a book is okay, depending on the subject matter, but I don't have the patience or the concentration skills required. I don't understand it. In high school I always got good grades – but that was only because I had a good memory. I usually can't follow the specific details of a plot [the one notable exception being Fifty Shades of Sh*t]. However I do trust my intuition as to what's going on in the subtext – and this assists me in comprehending the overall message of whatever text I happen to be reading. And so in that regard – my Grrrlfriends have always been impressed with my supposed ability to deconstruct the classics of the Western Canon. Nonetheless, I disagree with their optimistic analysis and have tried to impress upon them ..... that I understand little of what I read. Lately they've started to keep a closer eye on my behavior ..... they've observed my preference for *Anal Sex and The Sh*tty* type dresses and have written me off as a *Boss Bimbo* ..... *(Addressing The Grrrlfriends)* In the long run, since I couldn't absorb advanced intellectual concepts in a way that would enable me to sustain an academic career – I decided to stop reading books entirely and to start spending more time on my knees .....

Grrrlfriend One:
Spending more time on your knees? And what do you mean by that?

Jean-Nette (*winking*):

Oh cmon ..... you know ..... with men .....

Grrrlfriend Two:

No I don't know! What do you mean ..... *with men?*

Jean-Nette:

Well ..... I get on my knees ..... he stands up ..... and then we do things .....

Grrrlfriend One:

You *do things?* So what are you trying to tell me?

Jean-Nette:

Well ..... I'd love to tell you more ..... but I'm shy ..... and embarrassed ..... I had a very Puritanickal ..... you could even say Vicktorian ..... upbringing.

Grrrlfriend Two:

Do you spend time on your knees ..... because you get tired of standing up?

Jean-Nette:

Hmmmm ..... Well it goes beyond that ..... It's more like I just get tired of being myself. And so I like to pretend that I'm a kitty cat ..... I've always admired the Julie Newmar *Catwoman* from the original *Batman*[38] series .....I like to wear a mask like hers ..... and heels like hers ..... but not so many clothes ..... get the picture?

Grrrlfriend One:

You know you're driving me out of my mind with your mysterious implications and vague descriptions of ..... I don't know what!

Jean-Nette:

Oh ..... so I'm driving you out of your FUCKING mind?

Grrrlfriend One:

I didn't say that!

Jean-Nette:

I know ..... but I wish you had ..... because then I'd be more comfortable talking to you about

..... how I like to spend a lot of time on my knees

.....

Grrrlfriend Two:

Don't you worry about your knees getting dirty? What about when you go outside and everyone sees your dirty knees?

Jean-Nette:

In the places I go ..... there's special bathrooms where people who have dirty knees ..... can wash them off before they go outside .....

Grrrlfriend One:

What kind of places are those?

Jean-Nette:

They're clubs where men and women meet ..... usually late at night ..... to indulge in decadence of a non-monogamous variety .....

Grrrlfriend Two:

You mean like ..... a ..... 4 H Club?

Jean-Nette:

No ..... not exactly ..... there's more of a consensual adult sexuality thing happening. (*momentary pause*) .....Would the two of you like to gain more insight into my personal preferences?

Grrrlfriends (*in unison*):

Yes ..... yes ..... I think we would!

Jean-Nette:

Then listen to this tale of a girl who, as a teenager, wrote a story for her mother that was specifically designed to horrify her .....

Mother:

Oh my darling intellectually precocious daughter! What hast thou prepared for me on this joyous day? Willst thou share the spoils and influences of thy glorious literary treasures with me? How I doth encourage thee to express thyself with elaborate metaphorical sovereignty, with verses that remind one of the lilac and viburnum trees that hath drunk of April-

May rains and have thereby bloomed to their fullest potential and capacity! Can my daughter fulfill my wish of a dream that shall flourish as do the oft-bespoken paramours of the sun-golden realms of my imaginings?

Daughter:
Oh yes mother! That I can and that I shall! And now here is a tale that shall verily transcend all superlatives that have been heretofore ascertained by those who worship the sacred works of the Western Canon!

(The Daughter unfolds a piece of paper upon which her story has been composed and proceeds with her recounting).

Daughter:
..... Dat mornin I went tuh school, it was real nice out. I wore me a real purty dress. I was feelin damn good, I was mad phat happy when I walked up to thuh doors uh dat goddam school where I didn't do shit. Then I saw

dat bitch. I saw dat bitch dat think she all dat. But here what's funny: she ain't all dat! I said I'mma kill dat bitch. Didn't have no reason. Other than she got up in my grill. And then I went ovuh and jumped her and started poundin her head intuh thuh sidewalk .....

(*The Mother is speechless and clearly shocked. She rips the piece of paper from her daughter's hands*).

Mother (*shaking and practically hysterical*): Oh thou the daughter that I once hath loved! These are not the tales that I hath expected to be manifested by a young laidie in whom I had entrusted such high expectations; who would attend lectures within the hallowed halls of ivy-covered architectural masterpieces in which the best of all Amourrica Profoundan hopefuls doth gather and congregate to ameliorate their respective elevated understandings of our various historical and present day maneuverings! Whatever hast thou done? And so it now appears, that due to consequences arising from the inexplicably dark corners of a mind that should rightly have been locked within a fetid dungeon at an early age ..... I must expel thee! Never again shall I gaze upon that sweet visage of thine that verily hath sequestered reckonings of the devil's making. Shouldst thou ever appear within the confines of my parameters again ..... thou shalt be dispatched directly to Trailer Number Nine of the Marie Versailles Trailer Park in Oma-Pa, Nebulaska, Fartland, Amourrica Profunda ..... and then shalt thou comprehend mysteries, horrors and the blackest of nights ..... that no soul hath ever reported knowing! Or so it is said ..... I can say no more! Hélas! Away! Thou art banished! Thou are nothing to me! Get thee to a Non-ery! Get thee to thy hellish place and I shall remain rightly ignorant to thy whereabouts forthwith!

Jean-Nette:
And so Grrrlfriends ..... that's how I became what I am .....

Both of The Grrrlfriends continued to ask more questions, becoming ever more curious about Jean-Nette and her experiences. She finally suggested that the three of them should take a trip together – to visit Trailer Number Nine in the Marie Versailles Trailer Park. There was just one catch: The Grrrlfriends would have to be blindfolded prior to the journey. As The Grrrlfriends were too trusting – they consented. This made things much easier for Jean-Nette, as she would not have to reveal any information to them about being transported by means of Porn Keys and physioanimation ..... Once they'd all arrived at the Marie Versailles Trailer Park and were standing in front of Trailer Number Nine -- The Grrrlfriends became enchanted and mesmerized by Nancy Néant, who offered them some pink lemonade, which they gladly accepted. Before entering the mobile home, The Grrrlfriends looked back at Jean-Nette, with expressions on their faces that seemed to say ..... *We're scared but we're also excited and so we're willing to take this leap of faith.* Then The Grrrlfriends mounted the steps leading to Trailer Number Nine. Nancy Néant indicated the way to them with her outstretched left arm. The two of them stepped through the doorway of the mobile home and immediately encountered Nothingness .....

SEXY SEX HAIKUS
BY JEAN-NETTE THE JET LAG FAG HAG

SEX HAIKU ONE
Look at porn
Fill up emptiness
Days go by

SEX HAIKU TWO
In the dark
On my knees again
Cock worship

SEX HAIKU THREE
Love me not
You are shit to me
Turn to stone

THEY DISAPPEARED
BEHIND THE CURTAIN

When Grrrlfriend One and Grrrlfriend Two stepped though the doorway of Trailer Number Nine, they were enveloped in pitch black. It was if they'd been transported to the passageway-tunnel through which Katya Slalom-On, protagonist of Fan Crown's *In Search of the Boss Bimbo*, had been required to walk through to gain access to her top-secret laboratory. The Grrrlfriends were being compelled forward ..... by an unseen force. Suddenly they became aware of a small square of traffic light green far ahead of them, in the lower right hand corner of their respective fields of vision. This square of green light increased in size gradually as they moved ahead, becoming a rectangle, which gave them hope. And then the green light expanded exponentially and was all at once astonishingly bright, as if they were standing in front of a neon billboard in Thymes So Square, Puta Jork, Nueva Jork. The Grrrlfriends continued to move ahead ..... now they were flying over a blue green grid that resembled the landscape of *Tron*[39] ..... a geometric field that was simultaneously colorful and sinister. Without their being aware of any transition, their environment shifted once again by morphing into the light-show-travel coda of *2001: A Space Odyssey*[40]. The Grrrlfriends were now experiencing a re-creation of the final part of that film – *Jupiter and Beyond the Infinite*. The unseen force continued to pull them forward, which didn't keep The Grrrlfriends from enjoying their current *Sensurround* journey ..... both of them were too young to have tripped like an LSD-imbibing 1960s teenager. The Grrrlfriends faded out of that scene and faded into the next one ..... They were now hovering over *That Room From The End of 2001* ..... in which the astronaut protagonist in a red spacesuit, I-Don't-Care Dull-Eon, ages from gentlemanly senior citizen of leisure into a man on his deathbed. *That Room*, magnificent in spite of being windowless and desolate, featured a king-size bed covered with an olive green bedspread ..... a headboard, to which an oval-

shaped olive green cushion had been affixed .....
furniture upholstered in various shades of medium-
hued yellow-green ...... statues of classical nudes
appearing in small alcoves within pale blue and
periwinkle walls ..... and luminescent white floor
tiles framed by lines of gray. Then the black-brown
monolith appears ..... symbolizing who knows
what? The entire scenario represents the ultimate
nightmare of mortality, in which a frail and aged
gentleman has been abandoned by his fellow
man and will have to pass on without the comfort
of any human contact or goodbyes ..... It's the
room where no one wants to end up. Because
if they should – then they know that they'll die
alone there ..... with no guarantee of being reincarnated as a giant blue-white fetus, also known
as as *The Starchild* .....

And then The Grrrlfriends were confronted by
the *pièce de résistance* ..... a billboard covered
with messages ..... a post-post-post-modern installation, featuring several screens projecting outwards
at various angles. It was a presentation typical of
a contemporary Puta Jork, Nueva Jork gallery like

P. S. Lost. Written on its surfaces were poems by Jean-Nette the Jet Lag Fag Hag, verses written during Jean-Nette's downtime, that she hadn't been spending on her knees. These poems had been composed for The Grrrlfriends as a warning. The surfaces of the billboardesque-screen-instal- lation emitted a muted white light through trans- lucent Plexiglas; haikus had been inscribed upon those surfaces in bold black lowercase Helvetica characters.   But before The Grrrlfriends could read these verses, an announcement came on over the public address system. At first the sound was crackly; the quality was similar to that of Puta Jork's Megalopopolitan Transmit Authoritie. In other words -- incomprehensible. Fortunately the message was repeated three times and so by means of a concerted effort on their part, The Grrrlfriends were finally able to decipher the main gist of the announcement:

HELLO AND WELCOME TO EXTREME DISCO MATTRESS WHOREHOUSE. DO YOU LIKE SLEEP- ING? WELL THIS IS WHERE YOU'RE GOING TO

SLEEP FOREVER! (followed by wicked, reverberating laughter). AND NOW, WITHOUT FURTHER MOUNTAIN DEW, THE LOVELY AND TALENTED JEAN-NETTE THE JET LAG FAG HAG – WHO AS WE UNDERSTAND IT – SPENDS A LOT OF TIME ON HER KNEES – WOULD LIKE TO TELL YOU ALL ABOUT IT .....

End of message

Jean-Nette appears before The Grrrlfriends

Jean-Nette the Jet Lag Fag Hag:
For those of you who are confused about just what exactly you're doing here, when you thought you'd been reincarnated thanks to the Ultimate Buddhistic Detachment, here goes: (1) No, you're not in Dante's Crisco Disco Inferno of the Ninth Circle of The Vati-Cant; (2) No, you're not in Mimi Rogers' Purgatory of *The Rapture*; (3) No, you're not in *The Would Between the Whirlds* ..... You're in Extreme Disco Mattress Whorehouse! Which in this particular case is functioning as a Zone of Decompression

between the Blue Green Planet and the Nine Known Multiverses ..... But enough about that! I ain't no Alberta Einstein! I'm just another anti-social-networking narcissist zombie *actress on the mattress* and I want you to hear my poems. I want you to feel the love ..... the love that I pour into work. (*angrily*) I sure fuckin hope that you're gonna fuckin love my fuckin poems! And if you're one of those cynical bitches who doesn't believe that love exists, then (*screams with rage*) FAKE IT TIL YOU FAKE IT MORE -- FAKEBOOK FAKER ..... Can't you read the sign, Grrrlfriends? Here you go .....

Jean-Nette holds up a translucent Plexiglas sign emitting muted white light that states the following in bold black uppercase Helvetica characters:

CAUTION EXPLOSIVE BOLTS

Jean-Nette:
That's right Grrrlfriends – Extreme Disco Mattress Whorehouse is a very dangerous place! So watch your step!

JEAN-NETTE THE JET LAG FAG HAG

Jean-Nette proceeds to read her latest set of haikus

FUCK YOU HAIKUS
BY JEAN-NETTE THE JET LAG FAG HAG

FUCK YOU HAIKU ONE

Fuck you bitch
You dumb fucking bitch
Fucking dumb

FUCK YOU HAIKU TWO

And if you see this
Then you're walking around dead
You don't know you're dead

FUCK YOU HAIKU THREE

TV on
Fucking stupid cunt
Dull your brain

After this, The Grrrlfriends viewed a final presentation on the billboardesque-screen-installation

– one that cycled through all seven of the Shock-Ra colors, those being the colors of life [as opposed to the absence of life -- as represented by deathly white]. On the Shock-Ra spectrum screen appeared the following verse:

TOO RAW FOR HALLMARK
BY JEAN-NETTE THE JET LAG FAG HAG

Follow The Yellow Brick Ope-Ra
To The Emeryll Sh*tty
And to Ray-Kill Wraith of Light
Once within the Confines of the Emeryll Sh*tty
The Searcher will be brainwashed with
A Whitey's on The Moon Unit
A Lobotomie will be performed
Upon the Searcher to transform its mind into
A Hell-In of Goy Degenerate
Audience member

FIFTH DIMENSION DRAG QUEEN GATE-KEEPER

Dolores
The Day-Glo
Drag Queen

Dolores the Day Glo Drag Queen rocketed up from the depths like a demented super heroine. She was a study in phosphorescent blue, green and yellow. She was a re-interpretation of *Tron*. She was Ur-Saalaah the Sea Bitch, Crew-Ella de Parkay Villa and a re-versioning of every Puta Jork *Divine*-inspired gender collusionist below Fourteenth Street from the 1969 Stoned-Wall Riots going forward. She shot up from Nothingness like the Big Bang. She wasn't going to let Jean-Nette the Jet Lag Fag Hag take advantage of The Grrrlfriends, or of anyone else that she watched over in her not-so-under-the-radar, once-upon-a-time-it-was-an-avant-garde-community.

Dolores the Day Glo Drag Queen:

(*hovering in the ether -- soliloquy*) Wanna throw down? I take on all comers! Fuck with me – I fuck with you back! I'mma ain't no Poison Ivy League bullshit! Get the fuck out of here with your negativity – I got plenty of my own to share! You wanna fuck up my show? I'mma show you! Guess where you're goin – person who pushes against my petty tyranny ..... I'mma sendin you down into the *Drag Me to Hell* magma-caldera – the entrance to which lies beneath the Gersh-Loser Theatre where all of those Weak-Ed lovin girls hang out! Whadda they know? Honey! Themma so young! Wait till they're old, broken, damaged and bitter -- like those *Wounded of Fraud-Gay* queers, who I make fun of because they're younger than me – and because I can! And because non-breeders like their drag queens to be heartless ice cold bitches! That's how I work it honey!

(*She wails like a coal miner; the wailing morphs into echoing laughter*).

People get all sad and sentimental about how times are changin. Tough beans! Wake up and smell the ass-presso! That's reality! I didn't invent it. And frankly I can't deal with it. Except when outside forces threaten my Grrrlfriends. And then I rise up like Kali Shiva! Kali Shiva currently functions as the sole representative of my Third Eye Mind Koont Violet Anti-Shock-Ra Power Base! Okay maybe I contradict myself; sometimes I get my Goddesses mixed up and I'm not even sure what they represent ..... I'm drunk half the time ..... Career hazard! To obtain and maintain this level of semi-coherent brilliance – I write jokes on a strict schedule during lunch hour at my Puta Jork, Nueva Jork temp job .....

Dolores the Day Glo Drag Queen continues to rocket up from Nothingness, accelerating until she reaches the speed of light. Shortly thereafter she reaches the Zone of The Grrrlfriends. Dolores then decelerates and makes her presence known to them .....

Grrrlfriend One:

We are so glad that Dolores the Day Glo Drag Queen will annihilate Jean-Nette the Jet Lag Fag Hag! Jean-Nette has no idea that we are in cahoots with Dolores. Also we fooled Jean-Nette by pretending to be so naïve, so innocent, so inexperienced.

Grrrlfriend Two:

Jean-Nette the Jet Lag Fag Hag is hated and feared by all. She brings no joy into anyone's life. She is a taker who gives nothing back. She doesn't deserve to exist.

Dolores:

Girls -- Listen up! I've made a last-minute decision! Due to unforeseen circumstances that demand my immediate attention – I bequeath to thee, the two of you, responsibility for the destruction of Jean-Nette the Jet Lag Fag Hag! Please don't disappoint me! I have faith in you!

Grrrlfriends (*in unison*):

Yay! We despise Jean-Nette! We will pursue her to the ends of ..... wherever we find her. Consider your wish – and our wish – granted, Dolores!

Dolores:

But you must have proper huntin gear. How should I dress you? Who are your Amazonian heroes?

Grrrlfriend One:

Dress me as Femmy War! She takes on all comers!

Grrrlfriend Two:

Dress me as Baby GI Cheney! She kicks ass!

Girlfriends *(in unison)*: Bring it on – Jean-Nette! You bombastic, bellicose, belligerent Anti-Barbarella!

Dolores waves her wand, releasing a shower of red, black and yellow sparks, and The Grrrlfriends are immediately transformed into nefarious Hassassins – com-

plete with black ski masks, camouflage fatigues and jackets, and state of the art weaponry.

Grrrlfriends (*in unison*):
Hail Dolores! Listen to our song! An anthem that speaks to the pending accomplishment of our heroic deed! Here's to the annihilation of Jean-Nette the Jet Lag Fag Hag!

Ding Dong the Fag Hag dead!
The Fag Hag dead!
The Fag Hag dead!
Ding Dong the Fag Hag Bitch is dead!

Dolores the Day Glo Drag Queen vanishes into the ether.

JEAN-NETTE
THE JET LAG FAG HAG
RESOLUTION

Jean-Nette was running for her life on the Blue-Green Tronscape. She was dressed in a pink and blue scuba suit – colors that stood in direct opposition to her blackened, hardened heart, caused by years of soul-killing promiscuity. She was sweating, panicking, frantic. She knew that she was doomed but she had no choice but to move ahead. In any case – she would not surrender. The Grrrlfriends pursued her in a state of maniacal glee, taunting her all the way .....

Grrrlfriend One:

What the hell happened to Suzie the Phosphorescent Fuck-Monster, Jean-Nette?

Grrrlfriend Two:

Was she such a threat to you – that you had to make her disappear? We're going to hold you accountable.

Grrrlfriend One:

Did the two of you drag queen race on the perimeters of the graphically patterned planes of our current location – The Blue Green Tronscape?

Grrrlfriend Two:

Did she fall down into the *Go Ask Alice Rabbit Hole*? Are we to believe that she was pushed – or was it just an unfortunate accident?

Grrrlfriend One:

Did she travel through a Kubrickian-influenced *Interstellar* light show? Did she take some kind of hallucinogen? Was the whole thing just a Timothy Leary-Aldous Huxley-Federico Fellini-inspired acid trip?

Grrrlfriend Two:

Yeah baby! Back in the day when LSD was truly authentic!

Grrrlfriend One:

Or was she just flattened inside the singularity of a black hole?

Grrrlfriend Two:

Did she unknowingly consume the Oxycodone brownies unlovingly prepared by Chatty Kathy,

AKA "Chai-Tea Cathay", and in so doing – encounter The Great Unconsciousness?

Grrrlfriends (*in unison, in the chanting-style of a tragic Greek chorus*):

We cry out into the night for you / Suzie the Phosphorescent Fuck-Monster / Everyone thought you were just a dumb slut / No one realized that it was merely a self-destructive phase / They were too busy posting on Fakebook, Spacegrave and all of those other anti-social media networks / Whereas we always knew that when you grew up / You were going to win a No-Bull Prize / And put to shame everyone in your Fartland small town / Who scorned you for your low SAT scores / It's so tragic when people with advanced capabilities / Succumb to the Netherworld of Fucking Around ..... But to quote Georg Wilhelm Friedrich Hegel (him were a nineteen hunnerty Doucheyland guy that thunk reel good): *Animals are in possession of themselves; their soul is in possession of their body. But they have no right to their life, because they do not will it* .....

Grrrlfriend One:

It's going to be a good death, Jean-Nette.

Grrrlfriend Two:

Don't worry -- we won't kill you right away. We want you to enjoy your remaining time on the Blue Green Planet.

Grrrlfriend One:

Don't be disheartened, Jean-Nette! You still have a few minutes left!

Grrrlfriend Two:

And we'll give you some advance warning. We'll shoot off a finger, then an ear; and then we'll hit you in your shoulder blade so that you can keep running.

Grrrlfriend One:

This way you'll know that the hourglass is running low. We want to be considerate in that way!

Grrrlfriend Two:

And we actually have flamethrowers. This way we can set your head on fire like *Mr. Bill*.[41]

Grrrlfriend One:

Remember *Mr. Bill* from *Saturday Night Dead*? Back in the day when you thought you'd live forever?

The Grrrlfriends go ahead with their respective, lackluster impressions of Mr. Bill.

Grrrlfriends (*overlapping voices*):

Oh Noo! Oh Noo! Oh Noo! (*they laugh hysterically at their failed attempts to imitate Mr. Bill*).

Grrrlfriend One:

We're so sorry that you'll no longer be able to spend any time on your knees.

The Grrrlfriends shoot at Jean-Nette's fingers, ears and shoulder blades with their semi-automatic weapons.   Jean-Nette screams and struggles to keep moving ahead.

Grrrlfriend Two:
We're not going to shoot through any of your vital organs because we don't want you to stop running. We're working on Plan B. We'll get back to you very shortly.

Grrrlfriend One:
We're really enjoying watching you flee from us! We love the chase!

Grrrlfriend Two:
Is it time for the flamethrower, Sister?

Grrrlfriend One:
Yes, Sister. That moment has arrived.

Grrrlfriend Two:
Jean-Nette -- we just wanted to let you know that in a very short time – We'll set you on fire.

Grrrlfriend One:

If this makes it any easier – think of yourself as a self-immolating Buddhist monk who's experiencing *The Final Detachment!*

Grrrlfriend Two:

I love it, Sister! *The Final Detachment!* An upcoming Folly-Would film, in which Jean-Nette the Jet Lag Fag Hag won't be starring! (*more hysterical laughter*).

Grrrlfriend One:

Yet another dream deferred, Jean-Nette. You had your chance to grab onto the brass ring. Might as well make your peace with that – in light of your imminent demise!

The Grrrlfriends chant "Time For Death" eighteen times – then aim their respective flamethrowers at Jean-Nette.

Grrrlfriends (*in unison*):
She Shoots – She Scores!

Jean-Nette is hit with the flamethrowers. She screams and then starts to groan in agony. She crumples over, enveloped in fire. The Grrrlfriends shoot more flames at her. Jean-Nette the Jet Lag Fag Hag encounters The Great Unconsciousness.

The International Consortium Of Bullsh*t Artists Fakebook Fakers And Not-So-Hilarious Hacks

We who are assembled and gathered here to celebrate *Those Socks featuring Troll-Fame-Whorian Sucktion Cups on Their Respecktive Souls*, that one can receive by means of complimentary shaving kits on Business Class international flights, hereby definitively condemn the various finished and unfinished works of Noloso Chushingura, a delusional creative force who has been recognized by none of the *Known Producers and Promoters of Creative Works of the Early Twenty First Century on the Blue Green Planet.* We discourage his efforts due to his defiant resistance to conform to practices similar to those of artists who work within recognizably high profile, and therefore commercially viable, contexts.

This document has been delivered in complete secrecy, by a representative of Price Fight Water-Board-House to the Water-Board of Directors of *The Fine Upstanding Citizens Committee for The Ongoing Post-Millennial Review of Subliminal Values Contained within Artistic Works that Are Deemed to Be Suspect*, the purpose of said committee being to identify and to then subsequently expose anyone who seeks to exert undesirable influence on *Popular Culture* [as the term "popular culture" is generally understood by the majority of the Amourrica Profundan populace]; the aforementioned subliminal values being influences that stray from the continuing progression and / or evolution of the status quo [as the term "status quo" is generally understood within the framework of the current *Definition of Creativity as It Applies to The Ongoing State of Gentrification of The Blue Green Planet*].

Signed and sealed on this *The Twelfth of Never* by the following:

(1) Xavier Baba Au Rhum, procrastinator at Superfluous Disgruntlement Inc.;

(2) Alannah del Baywatch, non-ingenious ingénue / chanteuse;

(3) Sunni Dee-Lite, john of Stanley Thornside / criminally experienced bisexual hustler / last seen walking along Mulholland Drive, Lost Angelist, Kali-Porn-Eye-Ay, Amourrica Profunda;

(4) Earnest Femmy-Gay, founder of *The Worldwide Coalition for The Continued Proliferation and Propagation of Reign-Beau Flags*;

(5) Jean-Nette the Jet Lag Fag Hag, swinger / haiku poetesse / passive oral fetishist;

(6) Mr. Wisdom Lewis, also known as "Sir Ignorance Delusion", author of West African scam-spam letters distributed worldwide via email;

(7) Hannah Low-Rent, author of *The Origins of Fun*;

(8) Ah-Nice Ninja, black belt eroticist / exorcist;

(9) Break-Fast Parsippany, Joisey goil / Woman-Hattan wanna-be;

(10) Gym Part-Fascism, collector of custom made designer bags / infamous for being infamous / unreal fake-reality starlet;

(11) Jiffy Pesos, entrepreneur and son of Crew-Ella de Parkay Villa;

(12) Swiss Kisschrist, perennially costumed as a fetish nurse in the Annual Puta Jork, Nueva Jork Village Halloween Parade;

(13) Grigori Prick, also known as "Atta-Kiss Bitch", high end porn star;

(14) Gothra Schvulkopf, author of *The Sweetness of My Nutella-Filled Colon that Doubles as My Pantry*;

(15) Woofraymo and Warbullina Chushingura, aunt and uncle of Noloso Chushingura.

(16) ..... FYI BTW AKA TBD TBC .....

THAT
DESK
DRAWER
NOVEL

The Collected / Completed And Unfinished Works Of Noloso Chushingura

Unfinished Works

NOTES ON "IN SEARCH OF THE BOSS BIMBO"
BY FAN CROWN

PART III OF THE ROBERTA FAG-HAGDOM SERIES

Having read several novels by Fan Crown, including *Faggots and Screamers* and *Da Bitchy Koont* – I must confess that *In Search of the Boss Bimbo* cannot be considered to be Mr. Crown's best work. The lead characters (Pytor Slalom-On, Katya Slalom-On) possess an exaggerated kind of jaunty, gossip-by-the-water-cooler humor. Their personalities resemble comic book characters. Their reactions are caught cinematically, as if those reactions had been compressed into movie stills, snapshots or Selfishies. The above analysis also applies to the personage of In-My-Way Sappho, the Nipponese female director of the Office of Insecurity of the See-My-Way.

Conversely, the composite negative aspects of humanity reside within the villain Mal-Hack; a combination of metrosexual, spoiled brat, trust-funder and bad boy. He strays from the prescribed path and is ultimately punished in Hell. He is Lucifer the Fallen Angel; Beelzebub, Mephistopheles, Old Nick, Satan. Up until the disintegration of Mal-Hack, the book is a page-turner. But then the overly long and unduly moralizing coda begins and one realizes that -- although the author tries his best to appeal to, and to include, all of the faiths and philosophies of the Blue Green Planet – this book was ultimately written with the Amourrica Profundan Evilangelist minority in mind.

Mr. Crown is very effective at describing, as well as selling, Vashink-Tone, District of Amoebia, as a depository of architectural and hieroglyphic achievements of historical significance. Ongoing references are made to the enlightened quality of the Amourrica Profundan forefathers and to their efforts to create a transcendent legacy – as if to undo all of the damage done in recent years by the Free Radical Fright, The Tea Room Party and the Anti-Creatives. In its defense -- this novel ultimately refuses to be influenced by anti-intellectualism as well as by the coarsening of the culture.

In closing: an *homage* in the form of a hypothetical quote by Sepia Crooks directed towards Fan Crown: ..... *Fan, certo che sei un maestro. Pero cosa hai scritto non è un capolavoro – è solo un best-seller. Voglio sapere Fan – Cosa la maggior parte dell'umanità vuole fare? Essere o non essere?*

TREATMENT / SYNOPSIS

ANAL SEX AND THE SH*TTY / SEQUEL IN PROCESS

The quartet dress up in drag as the Woman-Son Grrrrls, complete with Xs on their foreheads, and travel to Book-Arrest, Roam-Mania in search of "The New Low Rent Urban Liberated Oi-Ropean Beau-He-Man Lifestyle". The group ends up in the hippest of wild and crazy places ..... a 1960s-style happening; a heavy metal black light poster party in a facsimile of the bedroom of a typical 1973 Amourrica Profundan male teenager; an open mike called "Radiation" attended solely by 1980s style Goths [who are dressed in black ..... and wear ghoulish black and white clown makeup on their faces].....The four girls then go on a trip to Hades, financed by the Ghost of Aristotle Onassis. For their voyage, they are each assigned specific roles: Sam-Hamster Bones as Clytemnestra, Scary Bad Snore as Medusa, "Miranda Wrongs" Snobbes as

Circe and Shut The Fuck Up Sweet Charlotte as Antigone. At a karaoke party on one of Aristotle's yachts they sing "Come Sail Away" by Styx in unison ..... Upon completing that number, their bodies explode, by means of spontaneous combustion, in the style of "The Fury"[42].

POETRY

INDIANA GAY PIZZA POEM

PERFORMANCE INSTRUCTIONS

Each Stanza is to be Intoned / In the Undulating Sing-Song / Of the Classically Well-Intentioned Slam Poet.

SCENARIO

[As the HOUSE LIGHTS DIM at the Orpheus Theatre, Beast Village, Puta Jork, Nueva Jork – The audience is beset by a hushed sense of reverence and wonder. Our Slam Poet appears from behind the red velvet curtain and steps into the CENTER STAGE SPOTLIGHT. The spectators are offended, yet fascinated, by his extravagant street wear. He begins cautiously – eventually reaching a crescendo of Hieronymus Boscar-acceptance-speech-style frenzy]:

I want to wrap myself up /
In a pizza-smeared reign-beau flag /
For my *gay* gay wedding to /
Some other intolerant he-bitch /
Even though I know that this /
Will never happen in a million years

CODA

And for dessert I'll submit /
To being pelted with /
Leftover *mousse au chocolat* /
In a patriotic re-enactment /
Of Woodstock 1969

BLACKOUT

The audience boos, cheers, storms out, falls asleep and exhorts the Slam Poet to go back into the closet .....

INDIANA GAY PIZZA POEM: THE SHOW closes after just seven performances at the Orpheus Theatre. Shortly thereafter -- the multi-talented, multi-genre and entrepreneurially-savvy Grizelda "Gender Diss-Illusionist" Girlie-Mann steps up to the plate, at that same venue, as the producer of THE LONGEST RUNNING SEMI-PROFESSIONAL OPEN MIKE IN HISTORY – that eventually becomes the longest running semi-professional open mike in history .....

STORY

ADD OLYMPICS

At the upcoming Attention Deficit Disorder Olympics, participants will not even show up for their specific events, due to their being distracted by the need to perform obsessive-compulsive rituals. Years of training, if the athletes have even managed to accomplish that, will go to waste -- as OCD rituals always take precedence over anything else. Nonetheless, the ADD Games will continue on with the hope that the participants will eventually arrive and compete in their particular events. Finally, the spectators will lose patience and tire of waiting for the athletes to show up. The ADD Olympic Budget Committee will run out of money, imminent failure will loom on the horizon and once again – there will be no success .....

PROSPECTIVE BOOK / MOVIE TITLES

BRUNNHILDE'S SELF-HELP BOOK:
HOW TO HOLD ONTO SIEGFRIED
AND GET THAT RING ON YOUR FINGER

¡HOLA KREUZBERG! ¡MAñANA DIE WELT!
A SPANISH-DOUCHEYLANDISH MEMOIR

THE NOT-SO-NOBLE HATE-FILLED PATH

FAUX CELEBRITY QUOTE

"Wannie jobbie job? Go get jobbie job. Wannie go trippie trip? Go trippie trip. You no too old to be trippie hippie if you wannie! ..... Wannie wifey, hubby, baby? All up to you. Ain't nobody stoppie you! Only you stoppie you! World don't give no fuck about you! Only you makie happen if you wannie!

-- Fuckminster Buller, Author of *Faiku, Saiku, Daiku* [The Fuck You, Sex And Death Haikus]

FINISHED WORKS

SELF-HELP BOOKS

ART IS DEAD: THE ANTI-BOOK

REVIEWS OF
ART IS DEAD:
THE ANTI-BOOK

BY NOLOSO CHUSHINGURA

"I didn't even read the book ..... but I happened to see Noloso in person at his book party. During his reading [which had not been sanctioned by the Embarrass Review, since he hadn't fucked around enough to gain sufficient status as a legitimate writer with street cred] ..... the zombie gallery whores were pushing and shoving to get to the wine and cheese trough ..... the place was full of mediocre delusional *poseurs* grasping and clutching for their fifteen nanoseconds of fame ..... it was a study in the kind of greedy, barbarous consumption that most likely includes a quick stop at the open-air vomitorium [that being any street in the Beast Village, Puta Jork, Nueva Jork where one chooses to throw up]. And all of this was quite deserved on the author's part, since what he'd written was an infantile, *pornographique* tragicomedy ..... a deconstruction of childhood and adolescent demons, that most people have already exorcised ..... that Mr. Chushingura chose to dramatize. Talk about regression! *Art is Dead: The Anti-Book* made me want to start sucking my thumb again!"

– Koontessa Klarissa Koontberger, author of *Drug-Induced Sexual Abuse by Mutual Consent — An Autobiography*

"..... In my dream, an angel in the form of Hannah Moan-Tanner Nikole Sniff appeared before me to proclaim: ..... *I'm watching "Twin Peaks"*[43] *in Spanish — I don't understand it because Oh My Goddess switched my brain and my pussy at birth ..... but the actors sure do funny things with their hands!* ..... Then I saw Dracula in a cylindrical dungeon with an open air skylight ..... a split second later, the rising sun came streaming down from above and he was incinerated [as occurs in *Interview With A Vampire*[44]]. I then spewed out a stream of fetuses from my womb ..... I felt cleansed. My point being: *Art Is Dead: The Anti-Book* was like a Girl Scout's diary of summer camp compared to that. A whiny treatise about asexuality, Puritanism and the curse of inherited wealth. Maybe the needle dick author will write a real book someday ..... *Don't let Henri Meunier's brass balls give you a concussion on the way out, Mr. Chushingura. Watch out for black ice, we wouldn't want you to trip and fall onto your botoxed bubble butt ..... We'll call you .....*

– Glorie-Whole "Gigi" Evil-Lynne Gigglefoock-Koontberger, author of *The PhD of Porn: An Auto-biography*

"..... I loved the pâté at Noloso's posh book release party; I guarded it zealously from my sibling Froompie for weeks afterward ..... we were starving at the time and it was all about survival of the fittest. I kept the pâté in a special freezer adjacent to mother's wine cellar. I sealed it in Tupperware, that was then covered with several layers of aluminum foil, and labeled it *venison* with masking tape and a Sharpie. I have always known that Froompie found venison to be revolting -- and so my battle had been won."

— Kroonchie Koontberger, underachiever and brother of Froompie Koontberger

"..... I found this riveting page-turner to be both offensive and disturbing. As I plumbed its depths, I shivered and burned like an evil flower ..... thanks to the crippling shame that this work of fiction released from within me. My favorite selection was a story that brought to mind a classic 1970s *pornographique* film ..... in which a clean cut suburban boy spends his summer vacation in a cabin by the lake, where he accidentally encounters some local rough trade, who threatens him by means of malevolent sexual aggression ..... In the end, by means of a clever ruse involving Quaaludes and Courvoisier, our clean cut suburban boy escapes from the clutches of the menacing hustler, and goes on to find great success in life ..... his crowning achievement materializing in the form of a No-Bull Prize for an interactive, interdisciplinary multi-media installation utilizing haiku, graffiti and Selfishies ....."

– Afreakuh Kaarl Bong, author of *Transmogrified Metastasized Indecencies*

"..... Sublime! Incandescent! Mentally-Challenged! ..... I was about to throw myself from the balcony of my $995,000 Williamspurge, Nueva Jork condominium ..... when I realized that I hadn't read *Art is Dead: The Anti-Book* yet! Once I'd finished perusing its passages, my suicidal depression had lifted and I realized that from that point on ..... Only my creativity would heal me! Thank you – Noloso Chushingura! You saved my life!"

– Cindy Cipro, graffiti artist, oxycodone addict and Outer Bore-Ho trust funder

TAROT FOR DUMMIES

ABOUT THE AUTHOR

Stephen C. Bird is a fiction writer and visual artist.   Other works by Mr. Bird include "Hideous
Exuberance" (2009, 2013); and "Catastrophically
Consequential" (2012). Mr. Bird was born in Toronto,
Ontario; grew up in Erie County, New York; lived for
many years in New York City and currently resides
in Canada.

ENDNOTES

FILMS, BOOKS, PUBLICATIONS AND TV SHOWS REFERRED TO IN "ANY RESEMBLANCE TO A COINCIDENCE IS ACCIDENTAL"

1. *Star Trek,* Gene Roddenberry, 1966-1969

2. *Superman II,* Richard Lester, 1980

3. *Satyricon,* Federico Fellini, 1969

4. *Fight Club,* David Fincher, 1999

5. *Nymphomaniac,* Lars von Trier, 2013

6. *300: Rise of An Empire,* Noam Murro, 2014

7. *300,* Zack Snyder, 2007

8. *Celebrity Deathmatch,* Eric Fogel, 1998-2002

9. *Avatar,* James Cameron, 2009

10. *Rear Window,* Alfred Hitchcock, 1954

11. *Juliet of The Spirits,* Federico Fellini, 1965

12. *Muriel*, Alain Resnais, 1963

13. *Sleeping Beauty*, Walt Disney, 1959

14. *The Bible: In the Beginning*, John Huston, 1966

15. *All That Jazz*, Bob Fosse, 1979

16. *Valley of the Dolls*, Mark Robson, 1967

17. *Robin Hood: Prince of Thieves*, Kevin Reynolds, 1991

18. *Der Baader Meinhof Complex*, Uli Edel, 2008

19. *The Omega Man*, Boris Sagal, 1971

20. *The Vein of Gold*, Julia Cameron, 1997

21. *Suddenly Last Summer*, Joseph L. Mankiewicz, 1959

22. *Natural Born Killers*, Oliver Stone, 1994

23. *The Rapture*, Michael Tolkin, 1991

24. *L'année dernière à Marienbad*, Alain Resnais, 1961

25. *The Ring*, Gore Verbinski, 2002

26. *Village of the Damned*, Wolf Rilla, 1960

27. *Burnt Offerings*, Dan Curtis, 1976

28. *Mulholland Drive*, David Lynch, 2001

29. *The Polar Express*, Robert Zemeckis, 2004

30. *Midnight Express*, Alan Parker, 1978

31. *The Dead Zone*, David Cronenberg, 1983

32. *The Twilight Zone*, Rod Serling, 1959-1964

33. *Willy Wonka and The Chocolate Factory*, Mel Stuart, 1971

34. *Nothing*; Laruocco, La Ruocco, La Ruoc&co. Enterprises and L A Ruocco; 2014

35. *Interstellar*, Christopher Nolan, 2014

36. *Drag Me to Hell*, Sam Raimi, 2009

37. *Logan's Run*, Michael Anderson, 1976

38. *Batman*, William Dozier, 1966-1968

39. *Tron*, Steven Lisberger, 1982

40. *2001: A Space Odyssey*, Stanley Kubrick, 1968

41. *Mr. Bill*, Walter Williams, 1976

42. *The Fury*, Brian De Palma, 1978

43. *Twin Peaks*, Mark Frost / David Lynch, 1990-1991

44. *Interview With a Vampire*, Neil Jordan, 1994

Made in the USA
Columbia, SC
11 January 2018